FIRE ON THE SNOW

As she entered the empty ballroom, Alida heard the sound of music.

Almost without realizing it, her feet carried her onto the polished floor on which the moonlight shone. She moved round the room, waltzing in an enchanted world.

Then, her eyes half-shut with the ecstasy of the moment, she no longer danced alone.

Round and round the Prince swung Alida until the music stopped.

She had dreamed she would meet such a man, that she would fall in love and her whole world would be changed because of it.

The Prince's noble good looks thrilled her. His kind words had touched her heart.

But Alida knew she loved in vain. For the Prince was the man her cousin was to marry . . .

BARBARA CARTLAND

Barbara Cartland

FIRE ON THE SNOW

BANTAM BOOKS
TORONTO · NEW YORK · LONDON

FIRE ON THE SNOW
A Bantam Book / January 1976

Published simultaneously in the United States and Canada

Bantam Books are published by Bantam Books, Inc. Its trade-mark, consisting of the words "Bantam Books" and the por-trayal of a bantam, is registered in the United States Patent Office and in other countries. Marca Registrada. Bantam Books, Inc., 666 Fifth Avenue, New York, New York 10019.

PRINTED IN THE UNITED STATES OF AMERICA

Author's Note

The Statute for the Emancipation of the Serfs was signed by Tsar Alexander II in 1861, a year later than the time this story takes place. The main characters are fictitious but the background comes from the reports of eye-witnesses. The cruelty, the Military punishments, the fear of the Secret Police, and the lighted gardens inside the Palaces are all accurate.

The Tsar's Aunt, the Grand Duchess Hélène, did suggest the idea of emancipation to her nephew and the way it might be achieved. The Michailow Palace is now the Russian National Museum.

Chapter One

1859

"Alida!"

The sharp voice was startling. Then there was the slap of a closed fan on a bent neck, which brought Alida to her feet with a little cry.

Deep in her book, she had not heard her Aunt enter the bed-room.

"Wasting your time, as usual!" the Duchess said harshly in her hard ugly voice. "If you have nothing to do, Alida, I will find you something. I have told you over and over again that I will not have you reading—filling your head with a lot of nonsense!"

"I am . . . sorry, Aunt Sophie."

"So you should be!" the Duchess retorted. "This is deliberate disobedience on your part, as you well know. Where did you get the book?"

There was a moment's silence before Alida said hesitantly:

"From the . . . Library."

The fan slapped her again, this time on her cheek. She took a step back, her small fingers creeping up to the burning mark.

"How often have I told you," the Duchess stormed, "not to take books from the Library? They belong to your Uncle, and they are not suitable for a young girl."

She saw the answer in Alida's eyes, and before she could speak, the Duchess continued:

"I know your father allowed you to read any of his books, but must I repeat, for the thousandth time, that I do not consider that either he or your mother

1

had any sense of responsibility, nor were they proper guardians for the morals of a young girl."

The Duchess accentuated the word "morals," and then, with an unpleasant twist of her thin lips, she added:

"That is of course hardly surprising, seeing in what profession your mother was engaged."

Alida clenched her hands together. She knew what was coming. She had heard it all too often before.

At the same time, it never ceased to disturb her, to make her yearn to spring to her mother's defence, to deny the cruel things that were said.

"How indeed," the Duchess continued, "could a creature who lowered herself to appear on stage know anything about propriety? A woman whom anyone could pay to watch, a woman who had none of the modesty and delicacy which should be an indivisible part of the female character."

"I must not answer back! . . . I must not!" Alida whispered to herself.

She knew only too well what would happen if she did.

When she had first come to live with her Uncle and Aunt two years ago, after her parents' death, she had not believed it possible that anyone could utter such cruelly defamatory accusations against her mother.

But she had learned through bitter experience that to argue or even reply only brought swift retribution in the shape of her Uncle's whip.

After two years of living in the Castle, Alida had acquired a self-control which gave her some small satisfaction because she knew it surprised her relatives.

Nevertheless, it was always hard to hear her sweet and gentle mother abused, and know herself too cowardly to go on fighting a losing battle.

"Books are for men," the Duchess was saying. "Women should sew, and a girl in your position, Alida, should make herself useful."

"I have tried to do that, Aunt Sophie."

"And so you should," the Duchess said. "You are a pauper! Do you hear me, Alida? A pauper! You live on the benevolence of your Uncle, and the least you can do to show your gratitude is to help me to the best of your ability, which unfortunately is lamentably ineffective."

"I do try, Aunt Sophie."

"Then put that book back in the Library immediately," the Duchess ordered, "and if I ever catch you taking one again, if I find you reading when you should be working, I promise you that your Uncle will punish you extremely severely."

Her eyes were cruel as she added:

"You may think, now that you are eighteen, you are too old to be whipped, but I promise you that if you behave like a disobedient child you will be treated like one."

"Yes, Aunt Sophie."

Alida picked up the book and moved towards the door.

"One moment!" the Duchess snapped.

Alida paused and looked back at her Aunt apprehensively.

Her large eyes in her small face were full of unshed tears, not only from the pain of the fan, which had left a livid mark on her cheek, but also because she always felt like crying when she heard her Aunt spit venom at her mother's memory.

Yet she realised that nothing she could say or do could change the bitter hatred that her Aunt and Uncle had for her.

"I came to tell you something which will undoubtedly greatly please you," the Duchess said slowly. "At the same time, your behaviour makes me wonder whether once again I should ask Mary to change her mind."

"Change her mind?" Alida asked in surprise.

"Your cousin is very kind and generous to you," the Duchess said, "although Heaven knows you do not deserve it. She has asked, Alida, that you should accompany her to Russia."

Alida stood very still, the expression on her face incredulous.

"To Russia?" she echoed, thinking she could not have heard her Aunt correctly.

"Do not repeat everything I say in that irritating manner!" the Duchess exclaimed. "Mary is to journey to St. Petersburg the week after next, when her approaching marriage to His Highness Prince Vorontski will be announced."

"Oh, Aunt Sophie, how wonderful for her!" Alida cried. "I hope she will be very happy."

"Mary will undoubtedly be extremely content to be the wife of such a distinguished personage," the Duchess replied. "And she has requested, I think misguidedly, that you should accompany her as her companion until she marries."

"And I am to leave with her . . . the week after next?" Alida asked.

"That is exactly what I have just said," the Duchess replied. "I cannot help feeling that Mary has made a great mistake. I would prefer that she should have chosen one of her friends. Perhaps Lady Penelope Berkeley, a charming, well-bred girl. But for some reason I cannot fathom, she wishes you to accompany her."

There was no doubt from the Duchess's voice that she found such a request extraordinary.

Alida's eyes were shining with excitement.

"It is very, very kind of Mary," she said, "and I will of course do everything I possibly can to be of assistance."

"So I should hope!" the Duchess said sharply. "There are not many young women who get such an opportunity. I can only pray, Alida, that you will behave yourself."

"Of course I will, Aunt Sophie."

"It is doubtful if you know the difference between right and wrong, considering the bad blood that runs in your veins," the Duchess remarked venomously. "But you will not be in St. Petersburg long, for the Grand Duchess Hélène, with whom Mary will be staying, will, I am sure, wish the marriage to take place soon after her arrival in Russia, in which case you can come home immediately by the cheapest and quickest route."

"Yes, Aunt Sophie."

The Duchess looked her up and down.

"I suppose," she said grudgingly, "you will require some more gowns, though goodness knows what your Uncle will say to such extravagance."

"I have very few that are wearable," Alida replied. "I have tried to alter some of Mary's old ones, but she is so much taller than I am."

"She is certainly distinguished," the Duchess said, "while you, Alida, are insignificant, as you should be. We will send for Mrs. Harben from the village and she can make you a few dresses for the morning, and perhaps one or two evening-gowns."

Before Alida could thank her she continued:

"There will be no time for more, even if we could afford the expense. Besides, no-one will look at you, and I hope you will have the good taste to efface yourself."

She paused to add impressively:

"Although you are styled a companion, you will be in fact nothing more than an upper-servant. You are there to obey Mary's commands, to see to her comfort."

"I understand, Aunt Sophie."

"I will send a groom to the village immediately to tell Mrs. Harben to come here this evening," the Duchess continued. "I think it would be best if all your gowns were in grey—a quiet, puritanical grey."

Alida was about to exclaim in protest, but she bit back the words even as they reached her lips.

'What is the point of arguing?' she thought.

She knew only too well that the Duchess intended to humiliate her, to make her feel subservient so that she would in fact be quite unnoticeable.

She longed for colour. Dresses of hyacinth blue or leaf green, primrose yellow or lilac mauve, even the pure white, which she should be wearing at her age as a debutante, would be a joy!

But she knew that her Aunt was right when she said she had to behave as a servant, for that was what they had tried to make her ever since she had come to the Castle.

It was seldom that she had a moment to herself.

It was unlucky that her Aunt should have entered her bed-room unexpectedly to find her reading a book that she had taken from the Library.

The fact that it was a Latin classic would not placate the Duchess, who thought that all reading was a waste of time, and that women should occupy their fingers and not their brains.

Nevertheless, at the moment, the fact that she had been forbidden ever to borrow a book again was not the catastrophe that it might have been, because, incredibly, she was to travel with Mary to Russia.

Alida had realised that for some weeks since a letter had been received from the Grand Duchess Hélène, Aunt of His Imperial Majesty the Tsar, there had been whispered consultations and a feeling of excitement which she could not exactly put into words.

She had known that something was being contemplated which concerned Mary, but no-one confided in her, least of all her cousin.

At the same time, because she was intelligent, Alida had been well aware that for some time the Duchess had been manoeuvring to arrange an important marriage for her only daughter.

The Duke of Berkhamstead, known among his contemporaries as the "Praying Duke" because of his sanctimonious air and much-professed propriety, had married the grand-daughter of His Highness Prince Fredrick of Reichenstein.

The Duchess never allowed anyone to forget her Royal descent, even though Reichenstein was a poor Principality and of little consequence in Germany itself.

But she was related, even if somewhat distantly, to many of the Crowned Heads of Europe, and she had set her heart on Mary obtaining an unparalleled social position, which befitted her outstanding beauty.

Unfortunately there appeared to be few eligible young Crown Princes or Heirs-Apparent among the European Hierarchy, and the Duchess had finally written to the Grand Duchess Hélène of Russia, who before her marriage had been a Wurtenberg. The answer had obviously been as gratifying as had been hoped.

Released by the Duchess, Alida ran along the corridors of the Castle.

She had been housed in the coldest and most uncomfortable wing, occupied by the senior-servants. Mary was in a more modern part of the building, with a large and comfortable bed-room and Sitting-Room looking South over the garden.

As Alida expected, her cousin was lying on a chaise-longue, as she invariably did after luncheon.

It was in fact the one time of the day when Alida was free from the demands that Mary fired at her unceasingly.

She entered the Sitting-Room and thought, as she looked at the girl lying against the silk cushions, her feet covered by an embroidered shawl, how lovely she was.

There was no doubt that Lady Mary Shenley's golden hair, china-blue eyes, and pink-and-white complexion, combined with almost classical features, made her a perfect example of English beauty.

Alida closed the door and advanced across the room to her cousin.

"Aunt Sophie has just told me the wonderful news, Mary! How kind, how very kind you have been in asking that I should accompany you to Russia! I can hardly believe it or tell you how overwhelmed I am."

"I thought you would be surprised," Mary remarked.

Her voice was hard and somehow not in keeping with the beauty of her face.

"I cannot think why you have asked for me," Alida said humbly, "but, whatever the reason, I can only say thank you."

Mary looked at her cousin with something like contempt.

"Can you really be so stupid?" she asked sneeringly. "I should have thought it was obvious that I have no wish to take a stranger with me! Someone who would be instructed to watch me, and expect me to behave as I have to do here—all that sanctimonious praying and psalm-singing!"

She gave an unpleasant little laugh.

"Papa has already given me my first wedding-present. What do you think it is? A Bible!"

Alida stood looking at her cousin without speaking, and Mary went on:

"If you come with me, you will do as I tell you, or else when I am married I will send you back to Papa with such a list of misdeeds that he will whip you insensible."

She paused and added:

"I am not taking you because I have any affection for you, Alida, but because for the first time in my life I am to be free, and I intend to enjoy myself!"

"But do you not enjoy yourself when you go to London?" Alida asked.

"Are you half-witted?" Mary asked. "How can I, with Mama permanently at my elbow, watching every step I take, making me repeat every conversation I have with a man?"

Her lips tightened.

"She frightens away anyone interesting with whom I might wish to dance! She never lets me out of her sight! If you think that is enjoyable, I can assure you I should find prison more acceptable."

"Mary!" Alida gasped. "I had no idea you felt like that!"

"Why should you?" Mary asked. "I have learnt to behave myself as Mama and Papa would expect when they are present. But thank Heavens, owing to Papa's arthritis, he cannot accompany me to St. Petersburg, and Mama cannot leave him!

"I am going to get away from them and I intend to employ to my advantage every moment of the time!"

Alida drew a deep breath.

"Oh, Mary, I wish I had known that you felt like that. It makes things seem better . . . for me."

"What do you matter?" Mary asked sharply. "Your goose was cooked from the moment your father married an actress."

"My mother was not an actress," Alida contradicted. "She was a ballerina. That is a very different thing."

"Not as far as Papa is concerned," Mary answered with truth. "She was a scarlet woman and you are well aware that, just as they will never forgive your father for leaving the Diplomatic Service to marry such a woman, so they will never forgive you for having been born."

"Yes, I know . . . that," Alida sighed.

"Therefore you may as well make yourself useful to me, and you can show your gratitude to me for getting you away from here, if only for a short while, by doing exactly what I want you to do."

"You know I am willing to do that," Alida replied.

"That is all I ask," Mary said, "apart from the fact that I shall expect you to help me with my clothes. Mama insists on my taking that ghastly old Martha with me."

She made an exasperated sound and continued:

"I am sure it is only because Mama knows Martha will spy on me and report everything I do! Perhaps I can have her quietly buried in the snow when nobody's looking!"

Alida gave a little laugh.

"I think that might be difficult, even in Russia!"

"I am not so certain," Mary answered. "I have heard that the Russians are pretty ruthless."

"What is Prince Vorontski like?"

Mary shrugged her shoulders.

"How do I know? I have never seen him."

"You have . . . never . . . seen him?" Alida could hardly utter the words.

"No, of course not," Mary answered. "It is a marriage which has been arranged by Mama and the Grand Duchess Hélène."

"But are you not frightened that the Prince may be old and horrible?"

"Do not be so ridiculous, Alida!" Mary replied. "Where Royalty is concerned, a marraige is always arranged. As it happens, I am told that Prince Vorontski is aged twenty-nine and extremely handsome. He is in fact the Grand Duchess Hélène's favourite relative, and, as you know, she is the Aunt of the Tsar."

"I hope you will be very happy," Alida said quietly.

"I cannot believe that the Prince will be more restrictive than Papa," Mary said. "Even if he is what Mama calls a 'good' man, I am sure we will not have prayers twice a day, and Bible-readings three times a week."

"I believe the Russian Court is very gay," Alida said.

"What do you know about it?" Mary asked rudely.

"I have heard Papa talk of Russia, and I have read many books about the country," Alida answered. "It is a land of great contrasts, immense wealth and terrible poverty."

"The poverty will certainly not concern me!" Mary said with a laugh. "The Prince, I understand, is extremely rich, and if he has a number of Palaces, which doubtless he has, then we need not interfere with each other unduly."

Alida gave a little gasp.

"Mary! What would Aunt Sophie say if she could hear you?"

Mary laughed again.

"Mama frightens you, does she not? And you have never learned how to handle her as I have. I can see her mark on your cheek. What did you do to annoy her?"

"I was reading a book," Alida confessed.

"I do not know why you annoy Mama and Papa by reading when they have forbidden it," Mary said. "I shall not bother with a lot of musty old books. I want to live my life! I want wonderful gowns, lots of jewels, and to have men—dozens and dozens of men—in love with me!"

"I am sure that will not be difficult, because you are so beautiful," Alida said in all sincerity.

Just for a moment Mary's hard blue eyes seemed to soften a little, but she said:

"What is the point of being beautiful when we sit

here week after week, month after month, year after year, and never meet any men?"

"You do go to London."

"For two months in the year," Mary retorted, "two months with Mama! And the year I came out Papa was there as well! I was lectured and prayed over every minute of the day."

She gave a humourless laugh.

"I was even locked in my bed-room at night in case some ardent admirer should creep up three storeys to get at me!"

As she spoke, Mary rose from the chaise-longue and threw the embroidered shawl which had covered her feet down on the floor.

"It makes me sick even to talk about it," she cried. "I knew what fun the other girls of my age were having. They had a chance of flirting when they went to a party, of listening to a proposal of marriage! Even of being kissed in an Arbour when they sat out at a Ball! I might just as well have had a squadron of soldiers guarding me!"

Automatically Alida picked up the embroidered shawl from the floor, folded it, and put it down at the end of the chaise-longue.

"It is all over now, Mary," she said. "You are leaving in the week after next."

"I know," Mary said. "Papa would not have let me leave then, were he not afraid of the Russian Winter. Oh, pray Heaven nothing will prevent my going!"

"I am sure it will be all right," Alida said optimistically. "Surely we are not travelling alone?"

"Naturally not, you nincompoop!" Mary replied, and now the note of contempt was back in her voice. "The Princess is sending a special Chaperon to England to accompany me, and His Majesty the Tsar has ordered the Minister of Naval Affairs to escort us."

"How very grand!" Alida exclaimed.

"I expect he is a doddering old Admiral," Mary answered. "We are travelling in an English Steamer as far as Kiel. There the Royal Yacht—the *Ischora*—will meet us and take us to St. Petersburg."

"I can hardly believe it!" Alida exclaimed. "I cannot credit that this is really happening! Oh, Mary, how can I thank you?"

"By behaving yourself until we leave," Mary answered. "If you put Papa in one of his rages, he is quite likely to refuse to let you come."

She saw the fear in Alida's face and went on:

"Then I shall have to have that spiteful little beast Penelope with me, or that horrible Elizabeth Houghton. Mama has always liked her because she soft-soaps her. I would not trust either of them, farther than I could throw them!"

Her voice softened a little as she added:

"So just for once, Alida, agree with everything Mama says. Be humble and respectful to Papa, and for goodness' sake help Martha to prepare my clothes."

"I will, Mary! I will!" Alida purred.

"I hope you are not coming with me looking like that!" Mary remarked.

She glanced as she spoke at Alida's faded and outgrown cotton dress, which, because the Duke would spend no money on her, had been patched and darned until the material could hardly stand the needle.

"Aunt Sophie said I am to have some new gowns made by Mrs. Harben," Alida replied in a low voice, "but she wants them to be in grey."

Mary threw back her head and laughed.

"Isn't that just like Mama?" she said. "You will have to carry your sack-cloth and ashes with you even when we go to Russia! Oh well, I do not suppose anyone will notice what you wear. They will all be looking at me!"

She gave a little sigh of satisfaction and walked across to the mirror to stand looking at her reflection.

"It is a good thing, Alida," she said, "that despite the fact that you are fair, as are all the Shenleys, we do not compete in any way."

"No, of course we do not," Alida replied. "How could we?"

"We are cousins, but you do not even look English," Mary stated. "You may have your father's hair, but your eyes have definitely a foreign look."

"My mother, as you well know, was Austrian," Alida said in a low voice.

"Oh well, I daresay she looked pretty enough when she was pirouetteing on the stage," Mary said. "I wonder how many lovers she had before your Papa came along, and she jumped at the chance of marrying an English gentleman!"

There was a moment's silence. Then, without replying, Alida slipped away.

She ran down the corridors back to her own room. Small, bare, and austere though it was, it was in fact the only sanctuary she had—the one place where she could be alone and free from the barbed remarks and jibes of her relations.

She shut the door, locked it, and threw herself down on the bed to hide her face in the pillow.

"Oh, Mama, Mama!" she whispered. "How can they say such things about you? How can they believe for a moment that you could be anything but good and as wonderful as I remember you?"

She wanted to cry, but somehow she forced herself not to shed tears.

She had cried so often, so long, after her parents had lost their lives. But now she had made herself exert an almost superhuman control over her feelings.

She knew that once she gave in to the continual bombardment of spiteful innuendos, foul accusations, and oft-expressed contempt for her mother, she would gradually become the weak, insecure, characterless creature they wished her to be.

It was her Uncle who had attempted to break her spirit on her arrival at the Castle.

She had answered back, contradicted, and defied him when he defamed her mother.

He had tried to beat her into submission and soon Alida realised that he enjoyed beating her, not only because he disliked her but also because he was revenging himself on his brother, who he believed had damaged the family honour in marrying a ballerina.

'How,' Alida asked herself, 'can I ever make my

Aunt or my Uncle understand? The love that Papa and Mama had for each was so overwhelming, so ecstatic, so beautiful that nothing else in the world was of any consequence.'

They had loved each other from the moment they met. They had married foreseeing the consequences.

They were well aware that they would be ostracised by their relations, that her father must leave the Diplomatic Service, and it would be best for them to live abroad, out of England.

None of this had outweighed the wonder that they had found in their love, the complete happiness of their marriage.

It was only Alida who must suffer for the sins of her parents, who must bear what almost amounted to a vendetta against her in the dark, cheerless Castle which had now become her home.

With an effort she raised herself from the bed and walked across the room to look in the mirror.

'Mary is right,' she thought. 'I do not look English!'

Her bones were very small and she had, like her mother, the figure of a dancer moving with a grace that was indescribable. Although her hair was fair—and, as Mary had said, all the Shenleys had fair hair—it framed a small heart-shaped face with enormous dark eyes.

Sometimes Alida's eyes were grey, sometimes when she was emotional they were almost purple in colour, like a pansy. Fringed with dark lashes, they formed a strangely arresting contrast to the pale gold of her hair.

There was something too in her features, perhaps the height of her cheek-bones, the tiny straight nose, the curve of her lips that could be entrancing when she smiled, that was also un-English.

'I am a little like Mama,' Alida thought, and felt a sudden warm glow of relief that she did not in fact resemble her father's relatives.

She gave a deep sigh. Ever since she had come to the Castle she had thought it the darkest, bleakest, unhappiest place she could imagine.

It seemed to sap her strength, to encroach upon her

menacingly like a dark fog, so that she could never be free of the misery of it.

To her mother, religion had been a joy and a comfort; to her Uncle it meant the harsh threat of Hell-fires in the hereafter and physical punishment in this world for those whom he considered sinners.

As far as Alida could understand, the Duke believed that all goodness was evoked only through fear.

She turned from the mirror and walked to the small window which looked North. She did not see the trees, the garden, or even the late September sun.

Instead, she was seeing a picture she had always had in her mind of Russia. Of snow, vast open spaces, of towers, spires, domes—and somewhere deep in the back of her mind, as if she half-felt that she dreamt it, a strange, tempestuous music which stirred the senses.

'O God,' she prayed, 'please do not let anything prevent me from going on this journey. Please let me escape, if only for a little while!'

"Have you not finished, Mrs. Harben?" the Duchess asked, sweeping into the Sewing-Room, where the village seamstress was fitting Alida with a grey cotton gown.

"Very nearly, Your Grace," Mrs. Harben replied. "It has been a rush to get so many things done so quickly."

"I am well aware of that!" the Duchess said sharply, "but her Ladyship leaves tomorrow and I do not pay, Mrs. Harben, for anything that is not completed to the last button."

"No, of course not, Your Grace. They will be done, I promise you. Even if my son has to deliver them at five o'clock tomorrow morning, when he goes off to work."

The Duchess's sharp eyes flickered over the gown which, drab and dull in colour, could not conceal the soft curves of Alida's young figure.

"I should have thought that the skirt of this gown

was unnecessarily wide," the Duchess said, as if determined to find fault.

"It is all the fashion, Your Grace," Mrs. Harben replied humbly.

"I am well aware of that, woman," the Duchess retorted, "but I would not wish my niece to appear ostentatious in any way."

"Of course not, Your Grace," Mrs. Harben agreed.
"Do you wish me to take a width out of the skirt?"

"There is no time for that now," the Duchess replied. "Mind the gowns are ready, Mrs. Harben, for I
will not pay one penny for anything that is not completed."

She went from the room as she spoke, holding her
fan in her hand, as usual, and Alida was half-surprised that Mrs. Harben had not been given a rap
over the knuckles.

Like herself, all the maids in the house were afraid
of the fan the Duchess carried Winter and Summer,
not because it ever seemed that she needed to use it
to cool herself, but because it constituted a weapon of
correction that she did not hesitate to use.

"Your dresses will be ready, Miss Alida," Mrs. Harben said as the door closed.

"I am sure they will, Mrs. Harben, and thank you
for working so hard on them. You must have stayed
up very late at night."

"I wish they'd been a prettier colour, Miss. It's a
crying shame that a young lady like you should be
garbed in such a dreary hue. Why, the last lady I
made a gown for in this colour was over sixty!"

"At least I have something new," Alida answered,
trying to look on the bright side.

"I'll tell you what I have done, Miss," Mrs. Harben
said in a conspiratorial whisper. "Since you've been so
nice to me, I've made you some muslin collars and
cuffs which you can sew on yourself when you get
away from here. They'll be real pretty against your
skin and will make the gowns seem not so drab."

"How very kind of you, Mrs. Harben!" Alida exclaimed.

"It's a present, like," Mrs. Harben said. "I'd like to give you a present when you're going on a holiday."

"It is a present I accept with every possible gratitude," Alida said.

She knew that even if she wished to do so, she would have no money to pay for the collars and cuffs.

"And for the evening-gowns," Mrs. Harben went on, still in a whisper, "I've cut them very much lower than Her Grace told me to do. Quite fashionable they are! And I found a bit of soft gauze in my work-bag that I used on a dress for Lady Sibley when she was in mourning."

Mrs. Harben glanced at the door as if she was afraid that the Duchess might reappear.

"I've stitched it around the neck of one gown," she went on, "and it looks quite pretty puffed over the arms."

"Oh, Mrs. Harben, that is sweet of you!" Alida cried. "I felt the bodices looked so bare that people would think I had forgotten something."

"There's something else, Miss," Mrs. Harben murmured in a voice so low that Alida could hardly hear her.

"What is it?" she enquired.

"I made Lady Sibley a new crinoline last week and she tells me to throw away her old one. It's a trifle bent on one side, but if you'd care to have it, Miss . . ."

"Mrs. Harben, you are an angel!"

Worse than knowing how dull and depressing her gowns appeared was the knowledge that she would be a complete frump without a crinoline.

Mary had a large one of whale-bone, which made all her gowns seem to swing alluringly and ravishingly from the waist.

It transformed the most ordinary dress into a Parisian creation worthy of the beautiful Empress Eugene, who had introduced the crinoline to the extravagant, pleasure-loving world of the Second Empire.

But the Duchess was adamant when Alida had hesitatingly asked if she could have a small one.

"Certainly not!" she had said. "They are not for someone in your lowly position. I do not approve of such an outrageous contraption for any lady, but Mary of course must be in the fashion."

She had looked Alida up and down, and added spitefully:

"Such frivolities are not for those whose lives must be spent in the expiation of former sins."

Now out of the big black bag in which Mrs. Harben brought the half-finished gowns to the Castle, she drew the whale-bone cage without which in England since 1857 no lady felt correctly garbed.

"Oh, Mrs. Harben, I could kiss you!" Alida cried.

"Hide it away quickly, Miss. Her Grace would never employ me again if she knew I'd given it to you."

"I will carry it to my bed-room under the gowns you've finished," Alida said, "and pack it at the bottom of my trunk. But how can I tell you how grateful I am?"

"You'll thank me, Miss, by having a good time," Mrs. Harben replied. "And mark my words, there's no-one in that there Russia who'll hold a candle to you, not when you looks happy, as if you were enjoying yourself for a change."

"I am sure I shall do that," Alida said. "It will be so wonderful to be abroad again. Besides, I have always longed to go to Russia."

"Well, now your dream has come true," Mrs. Harben said. "And perhaps you'll find yourself a nice husband, just like Lady Mary, and then you won't have to come home."

Alida did not answer. Her eyes had darkened. She was remembering a conversation that had taken place the day before.

They were sitting after dinner in the Salon. The Duchess was reiterating once again how lucky Alida was to be travelling to Russia when she might have stayed at home and made herself useful.

"I am very grateful, Aunt Sophie," Alida had said in her soft voice, with a note of excitement in it. "I am sure Russia is a very wonderful place and I know quite a lot about the history of the country."

"I hope what you know you will keep to yourself!"

the Duchess snapped. "Kindly do not try to force your opinions on other people or make stupid remarks that will cause Mary any embarrassment."

"No! No! Aunt Sophie. I will say as little as possible."

"Be sure you do not forget," the Duchess replied in a tone of voice which sounded as if she thought it unlikely.

Because Alida thought this a controversial matter, she changed the subject:

"Perhaps in a way I am luckier than Mary, as I am going there just as a traveller, while Mary is to marry someone she has never seen. If I were in the same position I would be very frightened."

"If you were in the same position?"

Her Uncle spoke unexpectedly from the other side of the fireplace.

Alida was startled. She had thought he was asleep.

"What do you mean," he enquired, "if you were in the same position?"

"I meant . . . if I was . . . getting married," Alida faltered.

"That is something which need not trouble you. You will never marry, Alida!"

She looked at him, her eyes bewildered in her small face.

"Never marry, Uncle Septumus?"

"No, never. I have thought it over, Alida, and I have decided that I could not allow the bad blood which runs in your veins to be perpetuated. I shall therefore, as your Guardian, not give my consent to your marriage now, or at any time."

He paused, his eyes on her pale face.

"You are fortunate," he continued, "in that you may stay here in the Castle and wait upon your Aunt. When she leaves us for a better world, I will arrange for you to spend the rest of your life in good works. I do not doubt there are Homes or Orphanages where your peculiar talents might be appreciated."

Alida did not answer.

She knew by the tone in her Uncle's voice that he was deliberately baiting her, hoping she would an-

swer him back, expecting her to protest, wanting her
to plead with him.

Instead, she bit back the words which rose to her
lips and said nothing. But inside herself she felt desperately afraid.

How could she bear it? How could she endure the
gloom, the unkindness, the misery of the Castle when
there was no hope of any reprieve? No chance of ever
leaving it.

Always at the back of her mind she had believed
that one day she would find someone whom she could
love as her mother had loved her father. That she
would fall in love, and her whole world would be
changed because of it.

She had dreamt about the man she would meet,
knowing he would not only be strong and masterful,
but intelligent and tender, kind and understanding.

He would be a man such as her father had been,
and yet exclusively her own. Someone she would love
instinctively as he would love her, because they were
meant for each other.

And now, as if her Uncle had sensed her innermost
thoughts, as if he determined to take away her last
vestige of hope, he announced his decision, knowing
that it would hurt her.

"You have understood what I have said?" he asked.
His voice seemed to echo round the room like thun-
der.

"Yes ... Uncle Septumus."

"So you realize that you will never marry? You are
not fit to be any man's wife, and I would not inflict
you on one."

"Yes ... Uncle."

"And when you are in Russia," the Duke continued,
"you will not mention the disgrace your father
brought upon our name. I would not have anyone
know that my brother could shame or humiliate me
as your father did in taking a light creature of doubtful morals for his wife. Do you hear? You will speak
of it to no-one!"

"Yes ... Uncle Septumus."

"It is something which is a blot on the family escutcheon," the Duke went on. "It is something which should never be spoken of to strangers, but of which you, yourself, will bear the burden and shame for the rest of your life."

The Duke stopped speaking. There was a silence, until Alida said in a voice devoid of all emotion."

"I ... understand ... Uncle Septumus."

Chapter Two

"It is really true! I am on my way to Russia!"

Alida found herself saying the words over and over again as she stood in the Saloon of the Steamer which was carrying them to Kiel.

Even after they had left the Castle, until the ship actually sailed Alida felt as if she were holding her breath.

There was always the chance that her Uncle might change his mind at the eleventh hour and she would not be allowed to accompany Mary.

The Duke had been in a querulous, disagreeable mood ever since the day of their departure had been decided until they said good-bye to him on the steps of the Castle.

Alida realised that it was in part because he was deeply disappointed at not being well enough to accompany his only daughter to St. Petersburg and see her married.

She could understand, too, that for the Duchess also it was hard to say good-bye and to know that when she next saw Mary she would be a married woman.

The Duke showed his feelings by being more disagreeable than usual, and choosing to make Alida the scape-goat.

Everything she did, everything she said, irritated him, until she was quite certain that he was working himself up to the point when he would insist on her staying behind.

When finally the carriages drove away down the

long drive and the Castle gradually receded into the distance, Alida felt quite faint with relief.

It had happened! She had got away! At least for a little while she would not hear that harsh and contemptuous voice, or feel the stinging slap of the Duchess's fan.

The Countess Orlov, who was their Chaperon, was an elderly woman whose husband had been Russian Ambassador to various Courts of Europe.

She had managed, with what Alida privately thought was excellent diplomacy, to calm the Duke's fears for Mary and to guarantee that under her chaperonage nothing untoward could possibly happen to her.

Count Ivan Benkendorf, the Minister of Naval Affairs, had met them at Harwich.

When Alida saw him she thought it was fortunate that he had not stayed at the Castle for the two nights before their departure, as the Countess had done.

Like Mary, she had expected an old Admiral, or at least an elderly Nobleman. But Count Ivan could not have been more than thirty, and he was a surprise from the moment he walked into their Sitting-Room in the Hotel where they were resting after their journey.

Extremely good-looking, tall and elegant, he kissed the Countess's hand with a grace that could never have been achieved by an Englishman.

Then, as she introduced first Mary and then Alida, his courtesy and charm made them all feel as if Russia already welcomed them.

"Count Ivan is certainly far from what I expected," Mary said to Alida when they had embarked on the *Maid of Hull.*

This was Messrs. Gee & Company's superlative Steamer which had been recently launched and glowingly written about in the newspapers.

"The Countess has been explaining to me," Mary went on, "that His Majesty the Tsar favours young men. In fact some of the most important posts are filled by men under thirty. Prince Orlov, who is only twenty-nine and a relative of the Countess, is President of the Imperial Council."

The two girls looked at each other. Then Mary with a little smile said:

"I am going to enjoy this voyage!"

'It is indeed enjoyable!' Alida thought the third day out.

But it was in a very different way from what she had expected. The sea became very rough from the moment of leaving Harwich. Martha had succumbed first.

As Mary was raging at having no lady's-maid in attendance, Alida struggled down the long corridor to Martha's cabin, which was in a distant part of the Steamer.

She found the poor woman being violently sick and quite incapable of rising from her bunk. She made her as comfortable as she could.

"I must get up, Miss," Martha muttered.

"I will look after Her Ladyship," Alida told her. "You lie still. I will tell the steward to look in whenever he can find the time, but I understand that nearly everyone on board is ill."

"I always did hate the sea!" Martha murmured faintly.

Leaving a basin beside her and placing a handkerchief soaked in Eau-de-Cologne on her forehead, Alida went back to Mary.

"I am afraid there is no chance of your seeing Martha until tomorrow," she said. "She is really very ill."

"Tiresome woman!" Mary remarked crossly. "I knew it was a mistake to bring her. Servants are all the same. They have only got to see a ripple and they tell themselves they are going to be sick."

"It is more than a ripple at the moment," Alida said with a smile, as everything slid from one side of the cabin to the other.

She was rather amused a little later when Mary said it was too rough for her to move.

"It is dangerous to walk about. I might easily break my leg, and that would be disastrous."

She looked rather pale and Alida thought privately

that in fact she was feeling sick. But she agreed that it was a sensible precaution and went in search of the Countess.

"I have no intention of moving from my cabin," the Countess told her.

Alida saw that she had already retired to bed.

"As it would be improper for you to dine alone at the Captain's table," the Countess went on, "you must ask the steward to bring you some dinner in the private cabin which has been put at our disposal."

"Very good, Ma'am," Alida said politely, and, having curtseyed, she left the Countess alone.

She was longing to go out on deck and brave the elements, but she thought it might annoy their Chaperon. So, having eaten a small meal alone, she retired to her own cabin with some newspapers which Count Ivan had bought for them before they embarked.

The next day was worse than the one before it.

The waves seemed to rise up like a green wall of water on either side of the ship, and they swept the decks with a fury which told Alida that however brave she might be it would be folly to go outside.

She went into the large Saloon thinking that perhaps some of the other passengers would be there and that it would be nice to have someone to speak to.

Mary, despite all her contempt of servants being sea-sick, was lying down with closed eyes, and Alida knew it was only will-power that was keeping her from actually being ill.

The Countess remained in her own cabin.

There was no sign of Count Ivan and Alida imagined that he was spending his time with the Officers of the Steamer.

She was therefore surprised when the steward told her that he was also in his cabin.

"Count Ivan cannot be sea-sick!" Alida ejaculated in surprise. "After all, he is a Russian Minister of Naval Affairs!"

The steward laughed.

"That doesn't say he's ever been to sea, Miss," he

said. "Foreigners aren't a sea-going race like us, and high-sounding titles don't save your belly from throwing up in a storm."

Alida laughed.

The steward was a bright-eyed little Londoner, and although she knew her Aunt would have found it extremely reprehensible for her to be chatting to him, she found his Cockney humour amusing.

She was soon aware that he had an Englishman's normal contempt for foreigners.

"It's always the same with them Russians," he confided. "Vodka and Turkish cigarettes, that's all they ever asks for. And of course caviar when they can get it!"

"Do we have any on board?" Alida asked with interest.

She had sampled caviar several times when she lived abroad with her father, and longed to try it again.

"No, Miss, oysters are our speciality, being really British, so to speak. But you will get plenty of that sturgeon's roe if you're going to St. Petersburg. Nasty greasy stuff, I always think, and not worth the money!"

Alida laughed again.

She was finding every moment of the voyage enjoyable, and each little incident seemed to make her laugh in a manner she had found impossible since her father and mother had died.

Now, standing in the empty Saloon, looking out at the waves washing over the bow of the ship, she felt that their wild exhilaration was echoed within herself.

"Good morning, Miss Shenley," a voice said behind her, and she turned to find the Captain, a large, bearded man, walking across the Saloon towards her.

"Good morning, Captain," she smiled.

"I must commend you, Miss Shenley, for being quite the most intrepid traveller I have aboard this voyage. A few more courageous souls have ventured as far as the Bar, but I see you are the only occupant of the Saloon."

"I came here to watch the sea," Alida said. "It fascinates me when it is as rough as this."

"I'm glad you enjoy it," the Captain said. "Most people find it unpleasant and intimidating."

Alida smiled. Then she realised that the Captain was not alone. A man had followed him in, a thin, rather cadaverous-looking your man with high cheekbones and dark, unhappy eyes.

He was looking at her and the Captain started, as if he had suddenly remembered his presence, and said almost apologetically:

"Will you permit me to present Mr. Tatkenski, a fellow traveller—Miss Alida Shenley."

The young man bowed, Alida curtseyed, and then when the Captain would have said something else, a member of the ship's crew approached him with a piece of paper in his hand.

"Excuse me, Miss Shenley," the Captain said as the man attracted his attention.

"You are Russian, Mr. Tatkenski?" Alida asked.

"No longer, thank God!" the stranger replied. "I am British—but I was born a Russian."

"I thought you must be," Alida answered.

She was surprised that he had spoken so vehemently, and now, as if he realised that he had been almost rude, he said apologetically:

"You must forgive me, but I should be unable to visit Russia now if your country had not been gracious enough to allow me to assume British Citizenship after living in England for fifteen years."

"And now you are returning to your home-land?" Alida said.

"I am going to search for my mother," Mr. Tatkenski answered, and his voice was harsh.

Alida looked at him and realised that there was a darkness in his eyes which told her he was suffering, and the sharp lines on his face seemed too pronounced for someone so young.

"When you left Russia, your mother could not go with you?" she enquired.

Mr. Tatkenski did not answer, and after a moment Alida said quickly:

"Forgive me if I sounded inquisitive, I am just interested in everything to do with Russia. You will realise that for me it will be a great adventure to see the country where you were born."

"Then let us pray," Mr. Tatkenski said, "that you will see only Princes and Palaces and not the real Russia."

"But the real Russia is what I would like to see," Alida replied quickly. "I want to meet the Russian people. I want to learn about them, I would like to know them. I wish to learn of their difficulties, their trials and tribulations."

Mr. Tatkenski gave a laugh which had no humour in it.

"What can you, a young woman from Britain, sheltered, cosseted, brought up in a free country, learn from a fear-ridden, ignorant Continent?" he asked.

There was so much pain and bitterness in his voice that Alida turned her face away from his towards the sea.

After a moment he said quietly:

"Forgive me. I had no right to inflict my feelings on you."

"It was no infliction," Alida said. "I want to understand."

She turned her face again to him as she spoke, and he looked at her as if he wondered whether she was speaking the truth. Then he said:

"I believe you are sincere. I would like to talk to you, if you will permit me to do so."

Alida gave him a little smile.

"It is unlikely that we shall be disturbed."

Mr. Tatkenski looked round and realised that the Captain had left the Saloon. They were alone among the plush-covered sofas, the gilt chairs, and the marble-topped tables.

"Shall we sit down?" Alida suggested.

She seated herself on one of the sofas and Mr. Tatkenski sat beside her.

She noticed that he was much too thin: his fingers were like claws, his cheeks were hollow, and she was certain that beneath his dark suit his ribs would be standing out as if from starvation.

As if he sensed her thoughts, he said:

"For many years I was forced to work beyond my strength. I was ill but because I wished to keep alive I had to go on working. Now I have come into a little money—not a large amount, but to me it seems a fortune. So I can now afford to make this journey."

"I am glad for you!" Alida exclaimed.

"It gives me a chance," he said, "of finding my mother again."

"You left Russia by yourself?" Alida asked.

Mr. Tatkenski took a deep breath.

"My father was a political prisoner," he said. "Do you know what that means?"

Alida shook her head.

"In the reign of Nicholas I, father of the present Tsar," he said, "two hundred fifty thousand political prisoners were banished to Siberia."

"So many!" Alida exclaimed.

"That is a conservative estimate," Mr. Tatkenski answered. "Many of them, especially the Poles, were flogged to death. The Russians use a knout which tears away the muscle in strips from the bone!"

Alida gave a little cry of horror: "Oh, no!"

"My father, I understand, was one of those who was murdered in such a manner," Mr. Tatkenski said dully.

"I cannot believe it!" Alida cried. "I know that the Serfs were badly treated in many parts of Russia. I have heard too stories of the punishments that were meted out in the Army."

"That is true enough," Mr. Tatkenski ejaculated. "My brother was a soldier. I learned from him that the blows from the Officers, flogging with birch-rods and sticks for the slightest fault, was normal practice."

"It seems incredible!" Alida murmured.

"Even in the Military Academy for Cadets, where only the sons of the Aristocracy are educated," Mr. Tatkenski continued, "a thousand blows with a birch-rod would be administered in front of the whole

School if a Cadet had been discovered smoking a cigarette."

"Is this really true?" Alida asked.

"It is true!" Mr. Tatkenski answered. "My brother told me that a Doctor would stand by the unfortunate boy and only ordered the punishment to end when he judged that the pulse was about to stop beating."

"But I thought that at least the Noblemen were pampered in Russia!"

"That is nothing to what the ordinary rank-and-file suffer," Mr. Tatkenski answered. "My brother was present when one of the common soldiers was brought before a Court Martial."

He paused to say slowly:

"The sentence was that a thousand men should be placed in two ranks facing each other. Each soldier was armed with a stick the thickness of a little finger."

"Please do not tell me any . . . more," Alida begged.

"The condemned man," Mr. Tatkenski continued relentlessly, "was dragged three, four, five, up to seven times, between the two rows, each soldier administering a blow."

He finished bitterly:

"The man died under the torture and the execution of the sentence was completed upon the corpse."

Alida put her hand to her ears.

"I do not . . . think I can bear . . . any more," she faltered.

"You wanted to know about Russia," Mr. Tatkenski said harshly. "That is why I tell you all these things. The English do not understand. They think they are compassionate and sympathetic, but a sick dog in your country gets more consideration than a thousand starving babies in Russia!"

He was silent for a moment before he said:

"I remember as a boy hearing that in one year the agents on the Borisovo Estate of Prince Radzi had beaten forty-four Serfs to death, blinded forty-two, and mutilated thirteen."

He looked at Alida's pale face and went on:

"Five years before I left Russia, in 1844, Hebrew

children of six years old and upwards were taken from their parents and sent to Regiments in distant parts of the country."

"But why?" Alida asked.

"They were required to embrace the religion of the Orthodox Church. Those who were old enough to refuse were horribly tortured to death."

"How bestial!"

"Thousands of Hebrew and Roman Catholic girls suffered a worse fate," Mr. Tatkenski continued. "They were assigned to satisfy the lusts of the soldiers."

Alida gave a little cry:

"But surely the people cannot . . . will not stand for such cruelty?" she asked. "I heard that in some places the Serfs have rebelled."

"With bare hands aginst gun-fire?" Mr. Tatkenski asked scornfully. "Do you realise that of the sixty million inhabitants of Russia, fifty million are peasants? And the Serfs number nearly forty million."

"Does that mean that they are in fact slaves?" Alida asked.

"They are completely and absolutely the property of their masters," Mr. Tatkenski answered. "A Serf can be bought, sold, or given away as a Christmas present!"

"It is inhuman!" Alida exclaimed.

"Of course it is!" Mr. Tatkenski agreed. "But who cares what happens in Russia? And how indeed can Europe know what is going on when Nicholas I, the last Tsar, controlled the newspapers, refused to build railways, and did his best to prevent all progress?"

"Surely the new Tsar is different?" Alida said.

"So I am told," Mr. Tatkenski replied, "but I will believe it when I see it! In the meantime, if my mother is alive I shall try to take her back to England."

"I will pray that you can find her," Alida said.

"It is more than likely that she will have starved to death," Mr. Tatkenski answered. "There are few people brave enough to help the families of political prisoners who have incurred the wrath of the Tsar."

"But you escaped!"

"I was smuggled out of Russia by some friends of my father who were fortunate enough not to be arrested when he was. My mother was too ill to travel, so they were obliged to leave her behind."

Alida heard the pain in his voice.

"They took me to England," he continued, "where I have remained ever since. But I have counted the days, the hours, even the minutes until I could go back. One day I shall have my revenge!"

There was something almost sinister in the way he spoke and Alida said quickly:

"You are an anarchist?"

"That is an English word for someone who wants a society without any government of any kind," he replied. "Call me an anarchist if you like. I prefer to think of myself as an ordinary man who rebels against injustice, cruelty, and sadism."

"Then you are right to feel like that," Alida said. "But I never think that more bloodshed and killing is justified in return."

"Then what is the answer?" Mr. Tatkenski asked.

"To try to bring enlightenment to those who have the power to change the existing order," Alida replied. "There must be able men in Russia who are aware of the social progress made in England and other European countries. Surely they will want Russia as a Nation to move with the times."

Mr. Tatkenski smiled.

"I can see you have an intelligence for these things," he said. "I promise you one thing, Miss Shenley, I will not throw any bombs until I have taken my mother to safety."

"When you have found your mother will it be difficult for you to get her out of Russia?" Alida asked.

"I shall have to smuggle her out!"

"You mean they will try to ... stop you?"

"If they discover who I am! The name Tatkenski is on the black list of the Secret Police."

"It sounds frightening!"

"There is no-one in the whole of Russia who is not terrified of the Secret Police."

"Then I shall pray that you can avoid them!"

Alida was not certain if he was joking or speaking seriously.

Because she felt so sorry for him she put her hand on his arm.

"I am sympathetic," she said. "I am, really. And if I can ever help you in any way, you know I would do so."

He looked at her for a moment. Then he raised her hand to his lips.

"I wonder if you will ever know how much it has meant to be able to speak to you like this, to tell someone of what has been bottled up inside me for so long. Now I feel an almost indescribable relief."

"I am glad if I have been able to help you," Alida said simply.

"You have helped me," he replied, and kissed her hand again.

She knew that he spoke with deep sincerity, and then she was aware that someone was watching them.

Glancing up, she saw Count Ivan at the other end of the Saloon.

He walked towards them and Mr. Tatkenski, realising that he was approaching, rose to his feet a little awkwardly and moved off without another word.

Count Ivan reached Alida's side.

"What was that man saying to you?" he demanded. "He had no right to kiss you hand."

"He was just thanking me for my sympathy," Alida answered. "He is one who has suffered greatly."

"He is a common creature of no consequence. I cannot understand why he is travelling First Class."

"I suppose he has the money to do so," Alida answered.

She was aware as she spoke that Count Ivan was surprised at the manner in which she had answered him. But he sat himself down beside her on the sofa and said politely:

"How is Lady Mary? I have been hoping she would be well enough to join us at dinner tonight."

"She is certainly better this morning," Alida answered. "I will try to persuade her to get at least as far as our private cabin."

"The Captain thinks the sea is subsiding," Count Ivan remarked.

He was very elegant in the manner in which he dressed, the way in which his hair was brushed back from his oval forehead, and the exquisite perfection of his cravat with its large, black pearl tie-pin.

He appeared to be thinking for a moment. Then he said:

"Try to persuade Lady Mary to dine tonight, but I think it would be best if we had our meal at the Captain's table. The private Sitting-Room adjoins the Countess's cabin and our voices might disturb her."

Alida looked at him quickly.

She was well aware that it was not consideration for the Countess which made Count Ivan decide that the Dining-Saloon was the best place for dinner.

Later, when she went to Mary's cabin, she found that the Count had already added his pleading to hers that Mary should make the effort to appear at dinner.

Sitting up in bed, her hair golden against the white pillows, and wearing a blue satin bed-jacket, she looked exceedingly lovely.

"Where have you been, Alida?" she asked crossly as her cousin came into the cabin. "I have been waiting here for you for hours!"

"I am sorry, Mary," Alida replied, "but I went to the Saloon to watch the waves. Count Ivan joined me there and he asked me to beg you to get up for dinner tonight."

"He has already written me a note," Mary said, "and I have every intention of doing what he asks. You had better unpack one of the other boxes. I want one of my prettiest gowns."

"Yes, of course," Alida agreed.

She hesitated for a moment and then said:

"Count Ivan has suggested that we should dine in the Dining-Saloon. He thinks that if we were in the private cabin we might disturb the Countess, who is still sick. But I am not certain if it would be the correct thing to do."

"Who cares if it is correct or not?" Mary asked. "Count Ivan is looking after us and we will do exactly as he suggests."

"Yes, of course," Alida agreed, and started to unpack the clothes that Mary required.

The sea was undoubtedly calmer by the time they went down the wide companionway to the Dining-Saloon.

It was decorated with a red carpet, shining gilt-framed mirrors, and was considered the zenith of luxury in the nautical world.

Count Ivan was already seated at the Captain's table, and as they walked across the Saloon every head was turned in the direction of the two girls, although in actual fact few travellers were yet brave enough to appear for dinner.

Count Ivan in evening-dress was even more impressive than he had looked in his day-clothes, and Mary, in a crinoline of blue-spangled tulle over crêpe satin exactly the colour of her blue eyes, was a perfect foil for him.

In contrast, Alida was acutely conscious that in her severe grey dress, which was only partially relieved by the gauze Mrs. Harben had sewn round the décolletage, she looked like a drab little grey pigeon beside two Birds of Paradise.

She realised a few minutes after she had sat herself down at the table that Mary and Count Ivan were completely engrossed with each other and no-one paid her any attention.

She looked round for Mr. Tatkenski, but there was no sign of him. The chair beside her was unoccupied, and she ate her meal almost in silence.

She was however too happy to be aboard the ship to worry about other company or to feel lonely.

When dinner was over Mary and Count Ivan went above to the Saloon and as they walked away from the table Alida took the opportunity to ask the Captain in a low voice if there were any books on board.

"Books? That's something I am not often asked for,"

the Captain replied. "But in actual fact we have quite a number. You will find them, Miss Shenley, in the card-room."

He smiled and added:

"You need not feel shy about going there alone, if that is your intention, as at the moment I feel it is still too rough for many people to wish to gamble their money on games of chance."

"Thank you very much," Alida said, and hurried after Mary and Count Ivan, praying that her cousin would not have missed her.

She need not have worried herself, for when she reached the Saloon it was to see that they were sitting together at the far end, deep in conversation, and she felt that to join them would be embarrassing.

She therefore asked one of the crew the way to the card-room, and having found quite an interesting collection of books she slipped away to her own cabin.

First she left a note on Mary's dressing-table, telling her to knock on the door when she came to bed, and she would come and help her undress.

She then got into her dressing-gown, settled herself comfortably on her bed, and started to read.

It was three in the morning before she finished her book, and when she looked at the watch her father had given her as a birthday-present she was astounded to find how late it was.

'Mary must have gone to bed without waking me,' she thought.

It was very unlike her cousin to show such consideration, and to make sure Alida opened the door quietly.

Standing in the passage outside the next cabin were Mary and Count Ivan. They were locked in each other's arms and Count Ivan was kissing Mary passionately.

Very gently, so as not to be heard, Alida closed her door.

It seemed impossible, she thought, that Mary should behave in such a manner, especially since she was in effect engaged to Prince Vorontski.

Surely Count Ivan should not abuse his position as

escort and Guardian of the English girl he was taking
to Russia.

Alida drew in a deep breath.

No wonder Mary did not want one of her other
friends to accompany her, if that was the way she intended to behave!

She must have fallen in love with Count Ivan, Alida thought. But what would happen when she met
the Prince?

Would it be possible for her to say that after all,
having made the journey from England, she had decided that the marriage should not take place and she
wished instead to marry someone else?

It seemed impossible that it should have happened
so quickly, and yet, Alida told herself, the Russians
were noted for being impulsive.

Count Ivan must have been infatuated with Mary
from the moment he had met her. Alida tried to look
back and remember any significant look or glance or
word that had been said after he had met them in the
Hotel at Harwich.

When they had travelled in the carriage, and when
he took them on board the *Maid of Hull* for their
journey to Kiel, she thought he had been very atten-
tive to Mary, but at the time it had seemed just ordinary politeness.

As far as she herself was concerned, Count Ivan
had treated her as she might have expected, as someone of no consequence. He had not assisted her into
the carriage or helped her from it.

He had even, she remembered, on one occasion
walked after Mary through a doorway, leaving her to
follow behind.

She had the feeling that while Count Ivan was very
good-looking and extremely smart, there was something not particularly pleasant about him. Perhaps it
was a hardness in his expression, or the occasional
sharpness in his voice.

"Maybe I am being unusually censorious," Alida
had rebuked herself.

Then Mr. Tatkenski's conversation came back to
her and she asked herself:

"Would Count Ivan behave towards his Serfs in such a manner as the Russian had described? Would he be prepared to inflict the cruelties which had made me feel almost sick as I listened to them?"

Because she felt certain that the answer to her question was affirmative, she hated to think of Count Ivan's lips touching Mary's.

About five minutes later there was a peremptory knock at the cabin door, and as Alida jumped to her feet Mary came in.

Closing the door behind her, she stood for a moment staring into the mirror. There was no doubt that her image was highly gratifying.

Usually Mary looked rather cold and statuesque, and there was a hardness about her face which was apparent to Alida if to no-one else.

Now she looked warm and glowing. There was a blush on her cheeks, her eyes were shining, and her mouth had the soft look of a woman who has just been kissed.

"Oh, Alida!" she said dreamily.

"You are happy?" Alida asked.

"I never knew any man could be so exciting!" Mary said. "He is wild about me! He is in love, he tells me, to the point of madness!"

"But, Mary," Alida exclaimed in dismay, "what are you going to do about it?"

"Do about what?" her cousin asked.

"About Count Ivan."

Mary gave a little sigh.

"I am going to hope that the night will pass quickly so that it will soon be morning and I can see him again."

"I do not mean that!" Alida protested. "I mean when you arrive in St. Petersburg."

Mary turned to look at her cousin in surprise.

"Why should I do anything?" she asked.

"But, Mary, have you forgotten that you are supposed to marry Prince Vorontski?"

Mary shrugged her shoulders.

"Then I expect I shall marry him. What does it matter as long as Ivan is there?"

"But, Mary, the Prince may find out!"

Mary gave a little laugh.

"I shall leave everything in Ivan's most capable hands. He admits he has been in love with many women, but never in his whole life has he seen anyone as beautiful as I! He says that from the moment he set eyes on me he was swept off his feet. He is madly, wildly, hopelessly in love!"

She gave a little cry.

"Oh, Alida, it is so marvellous and we have another seven days together! Could anything be more rapturous?"

"You must be careful," Alida said quickly. "What if the Countess should find out?"

"We can only pray that the weather is too bad for her to leave her cabin," Mary replied indifferently. "Anyway, I cannot worry about details. All I want is to see Ivan, hear his voice, feel him kissing me."

Her tone was almost ecstatic, and Alida said:

"Can you not marry him? Surely it would be best to tell the Prince the truth, and if he is a decent man he will not stand in the way of happiness."

"Marry him?" Mary gave a little laugh. "My dear Alida, Count Ivan is already married! Fortunately his wife lives in the country and seldom comes to St. Petersburg."

"Married!" Alida exclaimed.

She stared at her cousin incredulously before she said:

"Mary, if you knew this, how could you . . . how could you allow him to kiss you?"

"Allow him?" Mary echoed. "Ask me how I could prevent him! But what does it matter if he has fifty wives, as long as he loves me!"

"It is wrong," Alida said sharply. "You must see that it is wrong. It can only end in deep unhappiness for you both."

Mary laughed again.

"I declare you are as prudish and puritanical as Papa! My dear Alida, your job will be to cover up for us—to help me to see Ivan whenever I possibly can, and to keep the Countess from guessing what we mean to each other."

"How can I do that?" Alida asked nervously.

"It is for just this sort of reason that I brought you with me," Mary replied. "You will help me, Alida, or I will send you home on the next ship. Make no mistake about that!"

Her voice sharpened:

"You are here to be useful, and useful you will be! I have already told Ivan to send any notes he may write me to this cabin and not to mine. If either of us loses our reputation it will not be me!"

As Mary spoke she pulled open the cabin door.

"Come and help me undress," she said, "and stop preaching at me. I have had quite enough of that at home. I am not listening to sermons from you or from anyone else! Do you understand?"

"Yes . . . Mary," Alida answered meekly, and followed her.

Chapter Three

Alida stood on deck and watched as the Royal Yacht *Ischora* moved very slowly up the Gulf of Finland.

In the distance she could see the Kronstadt seeming to rise out of the sea, and ahead she could make out an enormous granite harbour and a long range of tall ships.

The smooth blue of the sea was literally covered with vessels. There were guard ships, men o'war, frigates, steamboats, packets, floating light-houses, and vessels of all sizes and of all countries.

It was all so colourful and beautiful that she drew in her breath appreciatively. Then a cross voice beside her said angrily:

"Will you go into the Saloon immediately and talk to the Countess!"

Alida turned her face to Mary and saw her cousin looking at her furiously. She realised suddenly that she was neglecting her duty, which was to keep the Countess from noticing that Mary and Count Ivan were seldom apart from each other.

They had been together all the time until they rounded the North point of Denmark and the stormy weather abated.

Then the sea became smooth and the Countess had risen from her bed, so Mary had commanded Alida to stay with her and keep her amused.

It had been hard not to stare out through the portholes at the picturesque and beautiful scenery. But Alida had done as she was told, and had slipped away only today, the eleventh of their voyage, because she was so anxious to watch their arrival in Russia.

In the distance over the bend of the Gulf she could just see tall gilt spires whose tapering points seemed to be lost in the blue of the sky. Also scintillating from afar there were domes and clustering cupolas covered with gold and silver or green-spangled with stars.

Alida was sure that the most stupendously burnished dome she could see was that of the colossal Cathedral of St. Isaac, so dazzling as to be visible, the Captain told her, at a distance of almost forty miles.

But because she must do as Mary told her she moved away from the open deck.

The *Ischora* was very luxurious. The cabin walls were of richly coloured woods, there were thick carpets, satin curtains, and the furniture was all very elegant and in exquisite taste.

Alida found the Countess sitting on a velvet sofa in the Saloon. There were great bowls of hot-house flowers to scent the air, and pictures on the walls which Alida recognised were by great Masters and extremely valuable.

The Countess looked up as she approached.

"Are you already bored with looking at our Russian Capital?" she asked.

"Indeed not," Alida replied, "but I thought that as you were alone I would keep you company."

The Countess smiled and there was a twinkle in her eyes, but she said nothing until, as Alida seated herself beside her on the sofa, she remarked:

"You can reassure yourself and your cousin that after years of living among Diplomats, I am like the wise monkeys!"

Alida's expression was startled as she went on:

"I hear no evil, I see no evil, and I speak no evil."

"I am sure that is very sensible," Alida replied in a low voice, "and it makes me feel that you are a friend."

"I would like to be your friend," the Countess said, accentuating the pronoun, "but let me inform you, my dear, that in Russia even the walls have ears!"

Alida looked at her in surprise as she went on:

"Everything that happens is reported to the Third Section of the Secret Chancellory, and Prince Vasilly Dolgoruky, who is Head of the Service, repeats every piece of information he receives, however small, to His Majesty the Tsar."

Alida knew that the Countess was giving her a warning not only for herself but for Mary.

She knew it was ridiculous to imagine that the Countess, who was extremely shrewd, should not have been aware of what was taking place between Mary and Count Ivan under her very nose.

'Thank you," Alida said quietly.

But even as she spoke she thought how frightening and in some ways how sinister it was! Already she was afraid.

She had been surprised, after the intimate way in which Mr. Tatkenski had spoken to her in the Saloon of the *Maid of Hull*, that she never saw him again. She wondered if he was ill, but felt too shy to make enquiries.

Besides, Count Ivan had made it very clear that he disapproved of him. Then late at night before they reached Kiel a note was slipped under her cabin door.

She picked it up and opened it.

Her eyes widened as she read the few lines scribbled hastily on the piece of unheaded writing paper:

I am leaving the ship tomorrow. Will you out of the kindness of your heart, which I sensed when we were talking together, tell no-one of the subject we discussed, or of my intended destination. If by any chance you are asked, please say you think I am going to Stockholm. I hate to ask this of you, but I know you will understand. Destroy this note.

There was no signature and Alida read the words again.

As if Mr. Tatkenski had told her in so many words, she knew that it was Count Ivan who was making it impossible for him to journey to Russia in the *Maid of Hull* as he had intended to do.

Sure enough, on the following day, when they had embarked on the Royal Yacht with much pomp and ceremony, the Count said, apparently casually:

"By the way, Miss Shenley, did you say good-bye to your Russian friend?"

Alida contrived to look puzzled.

"My Russian friend?" she queried.

"The gentleman whom I saw kissing your hand in the Saloon."

Alida forced upon her face an expression she hoped was one of bland surprise.

"He was a fellow-traveller to whom the Captain introduced me," she said. "He was deeply distressed over the death of his father, and when I commiserated with him he kissed my hand with what I thought was a very foreign effusiveness."

"Did he tell you where he was going?" the Count enquired.

Alida shook her head.

"I cannot remember for certain," she replied, "but I think he said he was journeying to Stockholm."

Count Ivan shot her a sharp glance, but she felt that she had convinced him and he was satisfied by her answer.

Mary now remarked sourly:

"That is just like you, Alida, to talk to strangers. You know quite well Papa would not approve."

"We only exchanged a few words," Alida said defensively.

"Then you did not speak to this man again?" the Count asked her.

"I never even saw him again," Alida said truthfully.

Now she found herself praying that Mr. Tatkenski would reach Russia in safety, and that he would not be circumvented by Count Ivan or anyone else.

He had been so sure that he was safe because he had British Citzenship, but Alida could not help thinking that if he disappeared his British Passport would be of little avail.

She sat with the Countess until the Yacht actually docked.

They disembarked, receiving every possible courtesy and attention and, because they were under the protection of the Imperial flag, being exempt from having to pass through the *douane*.

At last Alida had her first sight of the magnificent City which had been built at the command of Peter the Great.

The carriages bearing the Grand Duchess's Coat of Arms and drawn by superb horseflesh conveyed them from the Quay.

Alida sat beside the Count with her back to the horses, facing Mary, who looked a vision of loveliness in pale blue, and the Countess, very dignified in chocolate brown.

Alida had expected St. Petersburg to be big, but the colossal scale of the buildings made her feel that she had walked into giant-land.

The effect of the immense Palaces, enormous Squares, and wide streets was to make the people look like pygmies, and the carriages shrink to the size of nut-shells.

She stared out the windows, watching the traffic and finding that everything was exciting.

First she saw a pair of coal-black horses drawing a light, elegant chaise in which there was a Military Adonis with glittering casque and snow-white plumes.

Following him was an elegant brougham of English make and through its low oval window she could see an exquisitely beautiful occupant dressed in a flurry of feathers, satin, and jewels, which made her appear as if she were a creature from another world.

Then there was a crazy old cab on which a *yesvosgio*—a huge, bearded driver—was whipping the thin backs of two gaunt, angular animals.

Following these was a cart laden with oxen en route to the City slaughterhouse, and after that, heralded by a shout which sounded like "Take care, take care!" there was a ponderous patrician family coach.

It was drawn by four horses and driven by a veritable Colossus of a black-bearded Tartar enthroned upon a splendid hammer-cloth of black bear-skin.

It was all so thrilling that they had gone a long

way before Alida remembered to ask the names of the Palaces they were passing.

"These are not important," the Count said loftily. "When you see the Michailow Palace you will be really impressed. It is without a doubt the most important and luxurious building in the whole of St. Petersburg."

"Is it more impressive than the Winter Palace?" Alida asked.

"It was built by Tsar Nicholas for his younger brother, the Grand Duke Michael," Count Ivan answered, "and the Architect was an Italian called Rossi."

"Does not the Grand Duchess, now that she is a widow, find it too large?" the Countess enquired.

Count Ivan shook his shoulders.

"I imagine the Grand Duchess is content to have such a beautiful dwelling place," he answered.

"As far as I am concerned, no Palace could be too big," Mary smiled.

"You are right," the Count answered with a little laugh, "but the Michailow Palace is almost a town in itself. The Grand Duke Michael had his Officers living there, besides his Riding School, which is the finest of its kind."

"A Riding School?" Alida exclaimed.

"Fifty young men are instructed there," Count Ivan explained, "in all the sciences that are even remotely connected with the riding of horses. Their course of education lasts six years."

"That seems a long time," Alida remarked.

"And the Palace also contains a gigantic exercise-house six hundred and fifty feet in length. It is so large that a Battalion can manoeuvre in it, and two squadrons of soldiers fight mimic battles."

"It sounds fantastic!" Alida exclaimed.

As if Mary felt that her cousin was engrossing the attention of Count Ivan, she asked:

"What about the Ball-Room?"

"I want to show you that myself," Count Ivan answered in a caressing tone of voice.

Mary looked into his eyes. For a moment it seemed

that neither of them needed any further words with which to speak.

But already they had reached the Palace, and Alida saw that it was even larger than she had expected from what the Count had told her.

The Grand Entrance, richly adorned with sculpture, was supported by twelve large Corinthian columns and there was a great flight of steps leading up to the front door.

A number of servants in scarlet uniform ran down the steps to help them alight, and they were escorted up an enormous Grand Stairway to the first floor.

After walking for what seemed like miles along wide and magnificently furnished corridors, they came to what Alida realised were the private apartments of the Grand Duchess.

She had heard so much about their Hostess from the Duke and Duchess at home and even more from the Countess that, as often when one has a mental picture of someone, reality is a surprise.

The Grand Duchess was beautiful, but much younger in appearance and more vivacious than Alida had expected.

She held out both her ringed hands with a cry of pleasure when they were announced and hurried across the room to embrace the Countess before looking at Mary with a smile and saying:

"You are even lovelier, dear child, than I remembered."

Mary dropped her a deep curtsey, and the Countess presented Alida.

"I am so glad you could come with your cousin," the Grand Duchess said graciously. "Come and sit down. The servants will bring tea or wine, whichever you prefer, and you must tell me all about your journey."

The room was very large, with diversions and compartments making different little *éstablissements*. In one corner plants and flowers were grouped as in a Conservatory; another was railed off with rosewood and coloured glass for writing.

There were sofas and seats of all shapes, and books

which Alida noticed were in every language. One corner was fascinatingly reserved for pictures and miniatures. And everywhere there were flowers.

The room was very warm, and the warmth seemed to carry an exotic fragrance on the air so that everything was permeated with it.

The Countess was relating their adventures in the North Sea and describing the storm which had kept them all in their cabins, when the door opened and a man walked in.

Alida realised, even before the Grand Duchess rose to greet him, that he was Prince Vorontski.

He was without exception the best-looking man she had ever seen in her life. His features were almost classically perfect. His shoulders were broad, his hips narrow, and he moved with a grace which somehow she did not expect from a Russian.

He wore a Military uniform which accentuated his tall, lithe, and graceful physique. His breast was covered with Orders.

The Prince smiled at the Grand Duchess and raised the Countess's hand to his lips.

"Forgive me for not being here to greet you," he said, "but I was detained by His Imperial Majesty."

"And now I want you to meet Mary," the Grand Duchess said imperiously.

Turning to the English girl, she said:

"This, as I think you realise, is my cousin and my favourite relative—His Highness Prince Vorontski."

Mary held out a gloved hand as she curtseyed. The Prince took it in his.

"I have been eagerly looking forward to your visit," he said in a deep voice.

He spoke almost perfect English with only a faint, nearly imperceptible accent.

"I am delighted to be here, Your Highness," Mary replied.

They sounded, Alida thought, like two actors repeating the lines expected of them, and she could not help wondering if Mary's heart would respond immediately to the good looks of the Prince.

He was certainly far more handsome and altogether more impressive than Count Ivan.

"Now may I present Mary's cousin who is accompanying her," the Grand Duchess said.

She drew Alida forward.

"This, Vladimir, is Miss Alida Shenley."

Alida dropped her eyes shyly as she curtseyed. As she rose she found that the Prince was still looking at her.

"Although you are cousins, you are not alike," he said quietly.

"No indeed, Your Highness. We are very different in every way," Alida answered.

She could not help thinking a little wryly that he would be stupid if he did not realise very quickly how wide a gulf there was between them.

Mary's huge crinoline, under her tucked, ruched, and lace-trimmed gown with its small jacket, had taken up most of the carriage on their way from the Quay-side.

And although Alida had put on the small crinoline that Mrs. Harben had given her, she realised that it had done nothing to soften the harsh severity of her cheap grey gown, trimmed only with the white muslin collar and cuffs which the seamstress had made her as a present.

Her bonnet was devoid of all ornamentation save for two grey ribbons tied under her chin.

Inside Mary's bonnet, expensive lace softly framed her lovely face, and small curled ostrich feathers in shades of blue adorned the high crown.

"May I hope that you enjoy your visit to Russia?" the Prince asked.

Because Alida realised that he was paying particular attention to her, perhaps to put her at her ease, the colour rose in her cheeks as she answered:

"I already find everything fascinating, Your Highness."

The servants brought in chocolate, coffee, and wines on huge silver trays, and many delicious things to eat were handed round while they sat in a semicircle.

Mary was seated next to the Prince, and Alida saw
Count Ivan looking at them with a dark expression on
his face which obviously indicated jealousy.

"If you have no wish for more refreshments," the
Grand Duchess said a little while later, "let me show
you some of the rooms in the Palace before you retire
to your own suite. And I know that Vladimir will
want you to admire the Conservatory, which has become his special care since he came here to live with
me."

"I thought you had a Palace of your own," Mary
said in a note of surprise.

"I have several Palaces," the Prince answered. "One
in St. Petersburg, but it is very large and I have not
lived in it for some years. I also have a Castle in
Warsaw, but my main Estates are in the South."

He smiled at the Grand Duchess as he continued:

"My cousin has therefore been gracious enough to
give me one wing of her Palace as my own. It is certainly large enough—if not too large—for a bachelor."

As he spoke he looked at Mary, who smiled at him
beguilingly.

"I hope Your Highness will show it to me one day
soon," she said softly.

"I will certainly do that," he replied, "and you will
find it convenient that you can walk there instead of
having to take a carriage. But now let me show you
the Grand Duchess's Conservatory. It is indeed worth
visiting."

They passed through a number of magnificent
Salons.

Never had Alida imagined that so many treasures
could be collected in one place. The rooms were
enormous, but even so they seemed filled to overflow-
ing.

The first room they visited was a Great Gallery
with a magnificently painted ceiling and hung with
splendid paintings by Murillo, Canaletto, Guido
Renis, Reubens, and other great Masters.

Another room contained the most beautiful
Wouwermans, and there were many statues by Ca-
nova.

One Salon was lined with *armoires* filled with gems and curiosities, snuff boxes of every age and country, Imperial toys and jewelled *babioles*.

There were also costly caskets, ancient clocks, watches studded with diamonds and *objets d'art* of every sort and description set with precious stones.

"It is like Aladdin's cave!" Alida exclaimed excitedly and saw the Prince smile and turn his head to look at her.

The magnificence of the vases, jars, tables, and consoles wrought in porphyry, jasper, malachite, and lapis-lazuli were perfectly astounding.

There were superb porcelain vases of immense size, and so much red velvet and carved gold that it was impossible to take it all in.

'One day I must look at everything and try to find out the history behind such wonderful treasure,' Alida told herself.

Then they reached the Conservatory. It too was so enormous that it was like walking into an exquisite flower-filled garden. It might indeed have been part of Paradise.

The scent of the flowers was almost overpowering and their colours were unbelievable.

The Prince took them first to see his orchids, which the Grand Duchess told them he had collected from all over the world.

Like the other treasures, it was difficult for the mind to take them all in at once. There were orchids of purple and red, of yellow, green, and orange, orchids of exotic shapes and some that were strangely spotted.

Alida moved a little way from the party who were chattering about the flowers. The orchids were so beautiful, she did not want her impression of such beauty to be spoilt by superficial enthusiasm.

She stood looking at a little orchid which seemed different from the others. It was completely white and had five pointed petals.

The blooms were quite small, yet somehow they seemed to her to have a more exquisite grace and to be lovelier than any of the others.

"I see you are looking at my latest acquisition," a deep voice remarked beside her.

She looked up in surprise to find the Prince beside her.

"It is so very beautiful," Alida said softly, "and like a star."

"That is what I thought too," the Prince replied, "and I also think, now that I see you together, you are very alike."

Alida looked up at him in astonishment, but before she could reply Mary had joined them.

"Your flowers are lovely!" she said effusively. "The Grand Duchess has promised we shall see the Empress's jewels. That is something I am particularly looking forward to because I am told they are magnificent."

"They are indeed," the Prince replied courteously, "and I will also show you the Crown Jewels."

They moved away.

Alida remained looking at the little star-shaped orchid.

'Why did the Prince think that it looks like me?' she wondered. 'Perhaps because it is small and insignificant!'

But even as she gave herself the explanation she was sure, completely and absolutely sure, that it was not the right answer.

They moved back through another suite of fabulous Salons to the centre of the Palace and from there the Grand Duchess had them shown to their bedrooms.

A suite of rooms had been put at their disposal in the South wing of the Palace.

The Countess was to stay with them for only two days before she left to join her husband in Warsaw, but her room was as magnificent as Mary's.

Alida had a slightly smaller room, but even that seemed very large, and like the others it opened on to a Sitting-Room which was be-decked with flowers.

It was Alida who realised that every flower in the room was English and that it was in effect a compliment.

"Roses, carnations, lilies!" she exclaimed. "Do you realise, Mary, that the Prince must have chosen these especially for you? You must tell him you have noticed such a charming thought and thank him."

She realised as she spoke that her cousin was not attending.

Count Ivan had said good-bye to them when they retired to their rooms, but now Alida saw that Mary was holding a small note which he must have pressed into her hand as they said good-bye.

"He loves me!" Mary exclaimed ecstatically as she read what was written on the paper.

She and Alida were alone in the Sitting-Room.

"But, Mary, you will have to forget Count Ivan now that we have reached St. Petersburg!" Alida expostulated. "Remember that I told you the Countess's warning that there are eyes and ears everywhere! If you see the Count or if he writes to you, it is sure to be reported in the Third Section of the Secret Chancellory."

"I do not care!" Mary said fiercely. "I do not intend to give up Ivan to suit a lot of interfering busybodies. And if they do tell the Prince about us, what can he do?"

"Oh, Mary, do be careful!" Alida begged. "Supposing the Prince refused to marry you? Can you imagine how scandalous it would be or what your father would say."

Mary laughed.

"The Prince will not do that. It would cause, as you are well aware, a diplomatic incident. No, the Prince will marry me, and I intend to go on seeing Ivan, because he has said he cannot live without me and I feel the same about him."

She folded the little note and slipped it down the front of her gown.

"I am in love, Alida, and it is wildly exciting, especially because I am free of Papa. After all, the Grand Duchess has no jurisdiction over me."

"She is very fond of the Prince," Alida remarked.

"And I am very fond of Ivan," Mary laughed. "Come along, let us rest. I believe there is a huge din-

ner-party tonight at which I will meet the 'cream' of
Russian society."

There was time for a short rest before dinner, but
Alida found it impossible to sleep. Instead she lay
worrying about her cousin.

It seemed as if Mary, having escaped from the con-
strictions she had indured ever since she was a child,
was now prepared to be foolishly reckless.

'She will not listen to me,' Alida thought with a little sigh.

But at the same time she blamed the Count. He
was older and a married man, and should not behave
in such a manner.

'I dislike him! I dislike everything about him!' Alida told herself.

It was not only his behaviour with Mary that had
aroused her animosity, but also because she knew
that he was cruel and heartless.

Last evening, when they were having dinner on the
Royal Yacht, the Countess had said:

"I shall be interested on my return to St. Petersburg to discover how far the Committee discuss-
ing the emancipation of the Serfs has advanced in
their deliberations."

"Emancipation of the Serfs?" Alida exclaimed before Count Ivan could reply.

"Yes, did you not know?" the Countess asked. "The
Tsar has ordered that a Committee should be set up
to discuss means by which the Noblemen can give
freedom to their Serfs."

"Oh, I am glad!" Alida said. "I was not aware that
anything like that was contemplated."

"Only a few fools with Communist leanings have
suggested such a revolutionary step," Count Ivan remarked harshly. "His Imperial Majesty has been
pushed into agreeing to consider the matter, which I
assure you will get no further than the negotiating-
table."

"But surely Russian Noblemen must realise it is
wrong to own Serfs," Alida said hotly.

Count Ivan laughed unpleasantly.

"We call them 'souls,'" he sneered, "but I assure

you they are nothing but animals. They have no brains, and freedom, if they obtained it, would mean nothing to them."

"I can understand that," Mary interposed, "and I am sure no-one will want to surrender the 'souls' which are their own property."

"I have no intention of giving up mine!" Count Ivan said positively. "They are part of my heritage. They have a value that cannot be estimated and I shall oppose this ridiculous reform with every means in my power."

"I am sure you are right," Mary said admiringly.

With difficulty Alida bit back the argumentative words which rose to her lips.

The manner in which Count Ivan had spoken told her that he would indeed be an implacable enemy to any idea of reform.

Remembering the horrors that Mr. Tatkenski had related to her, she thought that the Count would be cruel enough himself to flog or torture any Serf who rebelled against him.

She had hoped that once Mary saw the Prince she would discard Count Ivan and forget what was only a ship-board romance. But it appeared now that Mary was more infatuated than she had realised.

Alida remembered the murmur of voices that she had tried not to hear night after night coming from inside Mary's cabin, and which sometimes had not ceased until the early hours of the morning.

She remembered the way they looked at each other and how Count Ivan made every possible excuse to touch Mary. Also she had often seen the fire in his eyes.

The Prince however was so much better-looking than the Count that it seemed impossible to Alida that Mary should not compare the two and whole-heartedly prefer the man she was to marry.

'Perhaps now that she has seen the Prince she will forget Count Ivan,' Alida told herself hopefully as she lay sleepless on her bed.

Then servants came to her room, carrying a round bath of silver which they placed in front of the open fire. After she had bathed, two maids then helped her into one of her grey evening-gowns.

The crinoline certainly improved its appearance, and on board ship Alida had let down the hem. But when finally she was dressed, she stared at herself in the mirror with almost a feeling of dismay.

The grandeur and beauty of the Palace had given her an idea of what she might expect from the Russian Nobility.

She had already learned from the Countess that the majority of the ladies at Court sent to Paris for their gowns and everything French was considered very *chic.*

"You will find that all the Russian Nobles and their wives speak either English or French," the Countess said. "His Majesty the Tsar had an English Nanny when he was a boy, and his children have a Scottish one. Because we have such a difficult language of our own, we find it easy to learn other people's."

"I should like to learn Russian," Alida said.

"That should not be difficult," the Countess replied. "You will find there are many ardent young gentlemen only too willing to teach you."

She smiled as she spoke and added:

"You are very lovely, child, as I expect innumerable people have told you already."

Thinking of the manner in which she had been treated by her Aunt and Uncle, Alida shook her head.

"Then if I am the first to say so, I shall certainly not be the last!" the Countess exclaimed.

But now Alida, staring at herself in a long mirror framed with marquetry, exclaimed despondently:

'Nobody will notice me!'

Mrs. Harben had done her best, but she was only a village seamstress. Alida had altered the hems and tightened the bodices of her gowns but she was well aware how drab they were.

Fashion decreed that the shoulders should be bare above a wide bertha of lace, embroidery, or tulle.

Alida's dresses had only a straight piece of the same cheap material, unadorned except for the small, almost insignificant piece of grey gauze left over from one of Lady Sibley's gowns.

The material that the Duchess had chosen was cheap and coarse, so that Alida knew she would look like a miserable little shadow walking behind Mary.

The latter would undoubtedly dazzle everyone to-night in her best and most expensive gown of white satin and real lace, caught up with bunches of pink rose-buds scattered with *diamanté*.

Alida gave a little sigh.

'I must not complain,' she told herself. 'I am lucky, so very lucky to be here at all!'

She did not realise as she moved away from the mirror that the dull grey gown made her skin look almost dazzlingly white.

Her hair was the colour of Spring sunshine, and in contrast her dark eyes, apprehensive and worried, were deep and mysterious as the sky at midnight.

She had turned towards the door when there came a knock. One of the maids opened it and brought across the room a silver salver on which there was a spray of flowers.

Alida glanced at them and saw that they were the little white-star orchids she had admired in the Conservatory—the flowers which were the Prince's latest acquisition, and which he had told her she resembled.

For a moment she looked at them incredulously, and then she realised that it was a generous gesture on his part to welcome her to Russia—to make her feel that she was one of his new "family."

She took the flowers and pinned them to the front of her dress.

They seemed to her to glow like a jewel against the dowdy grey material and echo the sudden light which appeared in her eyes.

Because someone had been kind to her she felt happier, and less apprehensive, humble, and insignificant.

She went into the Sitting-Room. Mary was already there, as was the Countess.

They both of them had nosegays. Mary's was of white roses, a perfect compliment to her English beauty, and the Countess wore two huge purple orchids which looked very elegant against her gown of oyster satin.

"Are you ready, girls?" the Countess asked. "The Grand Duchess told me that we are to assemble in the Ante-Room to the Banqueting-Hall. You both look very nice."

"Thank you," Alida smiled.

Mary did not answer.

She was in a hurry, Alida knew, not because she wished to see the Prince, to whom she would soon be officially betrothed, but to be with a married man whose note was at this moment lying between her breasts.

Chapter Four

There were over forty people assembled for dinner in the Ante-Room to the Banqueting-Hall.

Never had Alida seen such a glittering display. The women were, as she had anticipated, indescribably glamourous in their Paris creations, and beside them even Mary could only just hold her own.

Their crinolines seemed larger, their waists smaller, their décolletage lower, and the elegance of their dresses more decorative than Alida could have imagined, while their jewels were superlative.

Great ropes of pearls the size of birds' eggs, diamonds that seemed too big to be real, emeralds, sapphires, and rubies all glittered round long white necks or shimmered in dark hair skillfully arranged by Russian *coiffeurs* who had studied in Paris.

The men were mostly in uniform, their tunics of red, blue, or white festooned with decorations. And, quite apart from the splendour of their attire, they were in themselves exceedingly fine-looking specimens of humanity.

Nearly all of them were over six feet tall, with broad shoulders tapering to narrow hips. They would have been outstanding in any society.

The women led by His Imperial Majesty's sisters, Grand Duchesses Marie and Olga, were so beautiful that Alida found it hard to keep from watching them.

The Grand Duchess Hélène presented Mary and Alida to everyone present. The curtseys of the ladies, the bowed heads of the gentlemen, and the smiles with which they were greeted were very flattering.

At the same time, Alida was conscious that, after

one look at her dowdy grey gown, the ladies at any
rate had realised that she was not of any importance.

It was not that anything was said, nor was there
even a look of disparagement.

It was just some sensitive part of herself that was
aware that in an imperceptible manner they withdrew a little, and she was conscious of being rated
so insignificant that they need not trouble with her.

Only when the Prince greeted her did she see him
glance at the white orchid pinned to the front of her
gown, and there was a faint smile on his lips.

"I was ... honoured to receive them, Your Highness," she said in a low voice.

"It is the first time," he answered, "that I have ever
picked a blossom from one of my special plants."

She looked up at him wide-eyed before she said
humbly:

"I wish their beauty could have had a more worthy
background."

"There was nothing else that I could offer you," he
answered, "unless I had plucked a star from out of
the sky."

Alida stared at him in amazement, thinking that
she must have misunderstood what he had said. Then
he turned away and she saw him cross the room to
Mary's side.

They proceeded into dinner and Alida saw for the
first time the great Banqueting-Hall of the Palace. Its
painted ceilings and its white-and-gold-panelled walls
hung with magnificent pictures were even more impressive than she had anticipated.

What she had not expected was the magnificent
display of flowers which decorated the Banqueting-
Hall even more effectively than the priceless pictures
and furniture.

There were flowers everywhere, massed upon the
long dining-table among the gold ornaments, garland-
ing the pictures, and arranged in the most intricate
and beautiful manner in every corner of the room.

A whole Conservatory of flowers, it seemed to
Alida, concealed the Orchestra, which played very
softly at the far end of the Hall while they dined.

There was a footman in scarlet-and-gold livery behind every chair, and as Alida seated herself she thought how fortunate she was to be present at so colourful and so sparkling a party.

When she could take her eyes from the glittering guests and the ornaments on the table she realised that on her right was a man who was not in uniform and was nearly middle-aged.

There were threads of grey in his hair and she thought that he looked a little different from the other men seated round the table.

Because she had been taught that it was rude not to converse with one's partners at dinner, she asked a little hesitatingly:

"Are you a politician?"

Her companion laughed.

"No indeed," he answered, "I am a musician."

"A musician?" Alida exclaimed in surprise.

The gentleman must have realised that his reply was unexpected, because he said:

"I believe you have only just arrived, Miss Shenley. You realise that the Grand Duchess is not only a leader of society, but she has brought together here in her Palace the Arts and Culture of Imperial Russia. She has made it a centre for all artistic and literary men."

"How exciting!" Alida exclaimed. "I had no idea that I should meet such interesting people."

"Any author, painter, or sculptor is welcome at the Michailow Palace," her dinner-companion answered, then added with a smile, "and politicians, too!"

Alida felt excited. It seemed a long time since she had met men who could talk intelligently like those who had been her father's friends.

Her Uncle, the Duke, had no use for those whom he described disparagingly as "brainy chaps," and she said now to her companion with a note of excitement in her voice:

"Do tell me about yourself! What do you play? Or are you a composer?"

"I have composed many different sorts of music," he answered, "and the Grand Duchess, who inspires us with an unquenchable optimism, assures me that when I am dead I shall be acclaimed as great!"

He laughed as if to himself.

"Will you not tell me your name?" Alida asked him. "I am afraid I did not hear it when we were introduced."

"My name is Stroyensky," he answered, "and I hope that when I am dead you will remember that we had this conversation together."

"I shall hope to hear your music long before that," Alida smiled.

"Do you play yourself?" he asked.

"Not very well," she admitted. "But music always makes me want to dance."

Even as she spoke she realised that this was the forbidden subject.

Her Uncle would be incensed if he heard her speak of wishing to dance because it would recall what he termed the "bad blood" she had inherited from her mother.

"I am sure you are a beautiful dancer, Miss Shenley," Mr. Stroyensky said with a note of sincerity in his voice.

Because she felt a little shy at having almost invited the compliment, Alida turned to her neighbour on the other side.

He was an older man with a face which had once been handsome but seemed now set in hard lines.

There seemed immediately something almost familiar about him, and after they had spoken a few commonplace sentences she discovered the explanation.

"I hope my son looked after you and your cousin adequately when he escorted you here on the Imperial Yacht," her companion said.

"You are Count Ivan's father?" Alida asked.

"I am indeed," he replied.

"And you are a General," she said, glancing at the insignia on his uniform, the breast of which seemed almost obscured by decorations.

"I am the Commander of the Military Cadet College," he answered.

Alida felt herself stiffen.

She had not forgotten the horrors Mr. Tatkenski had described, and the manner in which the Military Cadets were punished.

After a moment, because she remembered that Mr. Tatkenski had not been in St. Petersburg for fifteen years, she said a little hesitatingly:

"Is the ... discipline at your College as ... strict as it was under the last Tsar?"

"Who has been talking to you of our discipline?" the General asked.

Then, as Alida did not reply, he went on:

"I believe in discipline. Young men need training to be good soldiers, and the first qualification is implicit and absolute obedience."

"Even if it is against one's conscience?" Alida asked.

"A good soldier does not require a conscience. It is not necessary for him to think," the General replied almost harshly. "All he needs to do is to obey orders, to jump to the word of command, and to be proud that he can serve his Emperor and his country."

There was a silence for a moment and then Alida said:

"Surely that type of training could make a man almost ... inhuman, a mere automaton, not a creature of ... flesh and blood."

"Men are flesh and blood when they face the cannon of the enemy," the General told her. "But unquestioning obedience to the superior minds of their Commanders can save their lives. However, a good Russian should always be prepared to die for his Holy Father."

That was the name, Alida knew, the Russian peasants gave to the Tsars to whom they attributed almost divine powers.

She realised that the General was speaking almost fanatically! Looking at the harsh lines on his face, she wondered how many impressionable and young men had suffered under his hands or been utterly destroyed by his brutal discipline.

It seemed to her that once again she could hear Mr. Tatkenski's voice recounting the horrors of the flogging that a culprit must endure often until death.

She gave a little sigh and, as if she could not bear to talk to the General any longer, turned with a sense of relief once again to Mr. Stroyensky on her other side.

"I have always heard," she said, "that the Russians are very musical. I shall hope to hear them sing while I am here."

"I am sure the Grand Duchess will take you to the Opera one night," he answered.

"I did not exactly mean the Opera," Alida answered. "I would like to listen to Serfs who sing, I am told, while they are working, and the river-boat men who have songs of their own. I would also like to hear the Russian Drinking-Songs which my father told me have a gaiety and a melody that one cannot find in any other country."

"I can see you are unlike the usual traveller who comes to St. Petersburg," Mr. Stroyensky smiled. "I shall not forget your wishes, Miss Shenley, and if it is in my power I will satisfy them all before you leave for home."

"I would like that very much," Alida told him.

They talked of music all through dinner, and because she was so interested Alida found herself hardly noticing the elaborate and exquisite dishes that were offered, in endless profusion to the guests.

It was only as dinner drew to a close that she realized she had behaved somewhat rudely to General Benkendorf on her other side. She had in fact almost ignored him. To make amends she said with an effort:

"You must be very proud of the important place that your son, Count Ivan, holds as Minister of Naval Affairs."

"I had rather he had gone into my Regiment," the General answered. "But he always preferred politics to Military strategy."

"I did not realise Count Ivan was interested in politics," Alida remarked.

"He is deeply immersed in them," the General replied. "At the moment he is helping Count Jacob Rosteray, the General Adjutant and one-time Chief of

Staff to Tsar Nicholas, to frustrate these fools who wish to give emancipation to the Serfs."

"You are of course against such . . . action," Alida said.

"It would be crazy and the ruin of many Noblemen," the General answered.

"And do you not think a solution can be found?" Alida asked.

The General brought his clenched fist down hard on the table.

"Never! Never!" he cried. "No traitor to all that is traditional in Russian history can be allowed to succeed in such a nefarious scheme! If they do, it will be over my dead body!"

He spoke with such violence that Alida realised she had provoked a storm.

It was with a sense of relief that she saw that dinner was finished and the Grand Duchess was rising to take the lady guests from the Banqueting-Hall.

"You see, we follow the English fashion, not the French," the Grand Duchess said as they moved down the long corridor.

"You believe in leaving the gentlemen to their port," Alida remarked.

Having lived in France, she was well aware that in that country the gentlemen left the room with the ladies.

"Exactly," the Grand Duchess replied. "I find, however, that although the men may enjoy the company of pretty women, they are always glad to have a few moments alone, when they can either be serious or have a freedom of speech that would not be permitted in our presence!"

She laughed a little mischievously as she went on:

"I have always been told that the worst scandals and the most spicy gossip are recounted as the port passes round the table."

The ladies were taken to three magnificently furnished bed-rooms to arrange their hair, powder their small noses, and to exclaim somewhat affectedly over one another's gowns.

"We are not dancing tonight, although there is a

Ball at the Winter Palace," the Grand Duchess said to Mary. "I thought, dear child, that you might be tired after your long voyage at sea. But next week you must be present! It is a special occasion and we are all to appear in Russian dress. I have already ordered a gown for you and one for your cousin, Alida."

"How very kind of you, Ma'am!" Mary exclaimed.

"I think you will enjoy the ball," the Grand Duchess answered. "It is always an amazing spectacle! The men especially look magnificent in their full regalia."

"I shall look forward to it," Mary said politely.

"Tomorrow I am giving a Ball here in your honour," the Grand Duchess went on. "I have decided it should be a 'White Ball' because soon the Winter will be here and St. Petersburg will be all white, and that after all is what foreigners expect of Russia."

Mary smiled, but Alida bit back a little exclamation of dismay.

She had heard of Balls in the past when every woman appeared in one particular colour. There had been Pink Balls, Black Balls, and Golden Balls which her mother had attended in Paris.

But she realised now that a White Ball meant that she had nothing to wear.

If her Uncle wished to punish her for her father's sin, he could hardly have contrived anything more subtle, she thought, than to condemn her to appear in the most elegant and glamourous society in Europe dressed like a waif from some charitable institution!

The Grand Duchess moved away, and for a moment she and Mary were alone at one dressing-table. The other ladies were not within earshot.

"What shall I do, Mary?" Alida asked in a low voice. "You heard the Grand Duchess say there is to be a White Ball in your honour, and you know that everything I have with me is grey."

"Then you will not be able to attend the Ball, will you?" Mary said indifferently, and moved from the dressing-table to mingle with the other guests.

Later in one of the grand Reception-Rooms the

guests talked while music from the Orchestra, which had played at dinner, accompanied their voices beguilingly through the open door of another Salon.

It was tempting, Alida felt, to listen to the music and not to trouble herself with conversation, but her father had always told her how tiresome it was to have guests who did not, as he put it, "pull their weight."

"It does not matter what you say, Alida," he had said to his fifteen-year-old daughter. "Just look interested and you will find that people will be only too willing to talk to you about themselves."

Now Alida found how wise this advice had been.

She had only to ask someone, either man or woman, to tell her what they did or even simply whether they lived in St. Petersburg, for them to talk animatedly about matters of which she knew nothing, but which nevertheless constituted a conversation.

The Grand Duchess was an exceptional Hostess and moved her guests round. Finally Alida found herself once again beside General Benkendorf.

"I hope you have enjoyed your first party in St. Petersburg, Miss Shenley," he said courteously.

"I have, indeed, General," Alida replied. "It is all so beautiful and so very grand that it is more like a fairy-story than I could possibly have imagined."

"I should like you to see the perfection of the manner in which my Cadets can march," the General remarked. "His Imperial Majesty has often commented on their precision."

"I should be interested to see them," Alida replied.

She hoped that he would not sense by the tone of her voice how much she hated even to think of the Military College, and the horrors that were perpetrated there.

"I will speak to the Grand Duchess," the General said.

He clicked his heels as he took his leave of her, and she hoped that she would never see him again.

At the same time, she had an uncomfortable feeling that, since he was Count Ivan's father, Mary might be interested in visiting the Military College.

The guests were beginning to make their farewells. The women curtseyed to the Grand Duchess, looking, Alida thought like beautiful swans.

She took a last look at the exquisite creations they wore of satin, tulle, lace and gauze, lamé and brocade, as with their jewels outsparkling the lights they moved from the Salon and down the Grand Staircase to where the servants were waiting with their cloaks and capes of fur.

Despite the fact that the sun shone warmly in the day, Alida realised that when it was dark it was very cold.

"We shall have snow," she heard an elderly lady remark prophetically as she descended the stairs. "I can feel it in my bones."

"Winter starts in October," her companion replied.

Almost last to leave the Salon was Count Ivan. He had been talking animatedly to Mary, and Alida saw her cousin reach out and lay her hand on his arm.

She seemed to be whispering to him until, as if he realised that he was conspicuous in being almost the last to go, he crossed the Salon to the Grand Duchess.

"I have enjoyed myself more than I can possibly express, Ma'am," he said. "Your parties are always intriguing and I am counting the hours until your Ball tomorrow night."

"I am delighted that you and your father can be my guests," the Grand Duchess said.

She sounded affable enough, but Alida had the idea that there was just a touch of stiffness in her voice, and there seemed a speculative look in her eyes as the Count bent his dark head over her hand.

The fact that Count Ivan forgot her altogether and left the room without saying goodnight did not perturb Alida in the slightest.

She was sure now that she really disliked him, and she also disliked his father.

'Surely,' she thought to herself, 'Mary will realise that it will be wise for her to make other acquaintances. There are so many men to choose from and all of them good-looking.'

She gave a little sigh.

'And one is better-looking than all the rest,' she added.

There had indeed been no-one in that gathering of fascinating men who looked as distinguished or as amazingly handsome as Prince Vorontski.

He returned at that moment to the Salon, having escorted the Grand Duchess's more distinguished guests to the front door.

"A most successful party," he said.

"You were pleased?" the Grand Duchess asked.

"Delighted!" he replied. "Who but you could mingle such a pot-pourri of opposites together and force them to enjoy themselves?"

Her eyes were twinkling as he went on:

"All the same I thought one or two of your guests might have a stroke when you introduced them to Nicholas Miliutin."

The Grand Duchess laughed.

"Surely they might have expected to meet him here?"

"Not at what was ostensibly a purely social occasion," the Prince answered. "But I daresay they will get over it, and it will give them something to talk about."

"Of that you can be quite certain!" the Grand Duchess remarked.

The Prince raised her hand to his lips.

"Good night, my most mischievous cousin, and thank you," he said. Then he turned to Mary.

"You have enjoyed yourself?" he asked.

"But of course," Mary replied.

He bowed conventionally and bowed again to Alida. His eyes met hers and for one moment she had the feeling that there was something he wanted to say to her.

Then as he withdrew from the Salon without speaking, she told herself that it was a ridiculous idea.

The Countess had retired to bed early, so the two girls, having said good night to the Grand Duchess, walked along the corridor to their own suite.

"What a dull evening!" Mary yawned. "I wanted to

dance. Ivan tells me it is usual in St. Petersburg to dance every night. It is only the Grand Duchess who has this tiresome idea that people want to talk."

"Did you not enjoy conversing with new people?" Alida asked. "I found them inspiring and very exciting."

"I wanted to dance with Ivan," Mary said petulantly like a small child. "Instead of which, we had to be careful. He has warned me that those women are 'all ears,' and there is nothing they would enjoy more than to say something spiteful about me."

"I am very glad Count Ivan has told you to be cautious," Alida said.

"He says he is thinking only of me," Mary complained crossly. "But I have a suspicion that he is afraid for his own reputation! He tells me his wife is very jealous."

"Perhaps she has reason to be," Alida suggested, but Mary did not reply.

They had reached their own Sitting-Room by now, and as Mary turned towards her bed-room door Alida said pleadingly:

"I would very much like to come to the White Ball which is being given in your honour. Will they not think it strange if I am absent?"

"I am sure no-one will notice whether you are there or not," Mary replied crushingly. "Papa gave me very little money for the journey and I certainly cannot afford to buy you a gown!"

She paused and added:

"After all, I have brought you to Russia. That should be enough for someone like you."

"Yes ... of course," Alida answered humbly. "I am very ... grateful."

Mary went into her own bed-room and shut the door sharply behind her.

Alida stood looking round the Sitting-Room.

There was a book-case on one wall which she had not yet had time to explore, and now she examined the books, and found, to her delight, that some of them were old favourites which she had not seen since she left Paris.

There were also many new books that she had longed to read but which had never been likely to enter the Castle.

She picked out three and carried them into her bed-room.

'How wonderful it is,' she thought, 'that here I can read without being told it is a waste of time! And here too, I can also have the chance of meeting interesting people like Mr. Stroyensky.'

Talking to him had brought back all too vividly the exciting and informative conversations she had listened to in her father's house.

She had almost forgotten how witty and humourous people could be. Or that, when they were well informed, they could range over a whole variety of subjects without being in the least pedantic.

It was very different from listening to the droning, gloomy, autocratic voice of her Uncle, laying down the law and allowing no woman, especially herself, to express an opinion, let alone argue with him.

'I could be happy here in Russia,' Alida told herself, 'if it were not for the cruelty.'

She put the three books down beside her bed.

She was just beginning to undo her gown when she remembered that the maid who helped her dress had asked if she would ring her bell when she retired to her bed-chamber.

"We'll come at once, *Ma'm'selle*, as soon as we hear it ring," the woman had said, who spoke a little French.

Alida had wanted to say that she always put herself to bed, but then she felt that the Grand Duchess would expect her to behave in the same manner as her other guests.

As her hand went out towards the bell-pull she heard a knock at the door. She thought that she must be mistaken, but it came again.

With a feeling of surprise she crossed the room. The knock had been so faint that she felt it could not have been a maid.

A little nervously she asked:

"Who is there?"

There was no reply and she opened the door. Outside, she saw a footman in red livery.

"Her Royal Highness would speak with you, Miss," he said in broken but just understandable English.

"Of course, I will come at once," Alida said.

She was surprised, but she thought that the Grand Duchess must have some instructions to give her about the morrow.

The flunkey led the way across the Sitting-Room and opened the door into the corridor.

He preceded Alida back they way she had come, not towards the Salon where the guests had been entertained, but to the Grand Duchess's private Sitting-Room, where they had been taken on their arrival.

He opened the door and as Alida entered the room she found that the Grand Duchess was alone.

"I am sorry to disturb you, my dear child," she said. "I hoped that you would not yet have retired to bed. I have a special treat for you."

"A treat?" Alida asked.

"There is a chance that Mr. Stroyensky will be leaving St. Petersburg either tomorrow or the next day. He is at the moment playing the piano for the Prince in his private part of the Palace and felt you would like to hear him."

"I would indeed!" Alida exclaimed. "How very kind of you, Ma'am!"

She paused and added with a smile:

"I think Mr. Stroyensky must have told you that, when we talked at dinner, I said I should so much like to hear him play."

"He is a genius," the Grand Duchess exclaimed. "But as yet undiscovered. I am determined that his music shall be brought to the attention of those who can place him where he belongs, in front of the public."

"He told me that you were a Patron of the Arts, Ma'am," Alida said.

"I try to be," the Grand Duchess answered simply. "Now come, I must not keep you up too long or you will be tired when there is so much to see tomorrow."

As she spoke, the Grand Duchess led the way from

the Salon and Alida saw that waiting outside in the
corridor there were two little sleighs on rubber
wheels. They were delightfully decorated and lined
with satin cushions.

The Grand Duchess saw her astonishment and
said:

"The Palace is so big that I find it exhausting to
walk to all the parts of it that I wish to visit, and so
these have been made especially for me!"

She laughed.

"As you can imagine, the children think them the
most amusing toys and race them down the corridors,
and even at times have the most fearful accidents in
them!"

"I am not surprised that they find them amusing,"
Alida exclaimed.

She seated herself in the sleigh, and the footman
who was pushing it set off at a sharp pace.

They must have travelled, Alida thought, some
hundreds of yards before they came to huge mahogany doors.

There were servants in attendance outside, but
these wore a green livery and Alida guessed that they
belonged to the Prince's personal staff.

The doors were opened and the Grand Duchess
and Alida were pushed into a big circular Hall.

There, having abandoned their strange vehicles,
they were led towards two other doors where there
were more flunkeys in attendance.

Alida could hear the piano being played before
they entered the room, and following the Grand
Duchess she found herself in a magnificently furnished Salon.

Seated at an enormous piano at one end she saw
Mr. Stroyensky.

Even to hear a few notes of his music was to realise
that the Grand Duchess was right and that he was a
master of his art. He stopped playing and rose to his
feet. The Grand Duchess put up her hand.

"Continue," she said. "Do not stop. We did not
wish to interrupt but to listen."

She seated herself on a sofa as she spoke, but, as

Alida would have sat down beside her, the Prince entered the room and came to her side.

"I want to talk to you," he said in a low voice. "Will you come with me?"

It was such a strange request that she looked towards the Grand Duchess for confirmation.

Almost imperceptibly the older woman nodded, and Alida followed the Prince across the Salon to a door opposite the one through which they had entered.

He opened it and let the way through an Ante-Room into a large and very impressive Library.

There were books stretching from the floor covered with Persian rugs to the beautiful painted ceiling where gods, goddesses, and cupids rioted in an Olympian Paradise.

There were also deep-red English-fashion leather armchairs in which a man could relax, and there was a huge log fire burning in the carved-stone fireplace.

All Russian houses and Palaces were kept delightfully warm with stoves which burned birch wood, but all the more fashionable buildings had at least one open fire.

While the Palace was lit with oil lamps, the light here came from huge candles set in carved candlesticks almost as high as Alida herself.

She looked round her, wondering if she would ever have the chance of looking more closely at the books and perhaps being allowed to read them.

Then, realising that she was alone with the Prince, she turned towards him with a look of enquiry in her eyes.

"Will you sit down, Miss Shenley?" he asked courteously.

Alida sat herself on one side of the fireplace and he sat opposite her.

He seemed very much at his ease, and yet, perhaps because she was particularly sensitive to other people's feelings, she had the idea that he was trying to find words in which to speak to her.

There did not seem to her to be anything she could say, so she waited.

After a moment the Prince said slowly:

"I understand that on board the ship which carried you as far as Kiel you met a man called Tatkenski."

Alida looked at him in astonishment. Whatever else she had expected him to say to her, it was not this.

There was a moment's pause before she replied warily:

"Yes ... there was a man of that ... name on ... board."

"You talked with him?"

"We were alone in the ... Saloon during the ... storm," Alida said slowly, "and after the Captain had introduced us ... we exchanged a few ... commonplaces."

"Did he tell you where he was going?"

Alida stiffened.

"Why should you want to know? What has it to do with you?" she asked quickly.

Then all the horror of the things Mr. Tatkenski had described to her, and the confirmation of them she had received at dinner from the General, came flooding into her mind like something overwhelming and evil.

Without considering her words, she went on angrily:

"Mr. Tatkenski is a British Citizen. He has the right, carrying a British Passport, to travel anywhere in the world. Why should you concern yourself with his movements unless, like other people, you wish to visit upon him the sins of his father?"

She drew in her breath sharply before she continued:

"Have you any idea what it is like to be punished for crimes you have not committed? To be frighteningly aware that people hate and despise you for nothing you can help or prevent?"

The Prince did not answer. His eyes were on her face as Alida, losing all sense of caution, went on:

"I had been told that Russians were cruel, but I did not know how cruel! I did not realise that in this day and age men were still flogged until they were insensible. Do you know what it is like to be beaten?"

Her voice dropped and she said almost as if she spoke to herself:

"At first you are proud and believe you can bear the pain, that you can defy the person who assaults you! Then gradually you find yourself weakening. You know you are being humiliated. You know that your pride is going ... your will-power is sapped."

Her voice dropped to a whisper.

"Then you hear someone screaming ... screaming ... screaming ... and it is ... yourself!"

Alida's voice broke on a sob before she said angrily:

"Mr. Tatkenski has gone to Sweden. You will not find him. I pray that you will never find him and he will remain free! Free from all the cruelty that is ... Russia."

She felt the tears fill her eyes. Without thinking, without considering what she was doing, she rose to her feet and ran across the room.

She pulled open the door, rushed through the Ante-Room, and entered the Salon where Mr. Stroyensky was still playing.

Her breath was coming sharply between her lips, and as she ran the tears spilled from her eyes onto her cheeks.

She stood trembling just inside the door, realising what she had said and how in fact she had insulted the Prince! Then she saw the Grand Duchess hold out her hand.

"What has happened, child? What has upset you?" she asked.

Slowly Alida walked towards her. Without conscious thought, she put her hand into the Grand Duchess's and felt the warmth of her clasp.

The older woman drew her down beside her on the sofa.

"Why are you crying?" she asked gently.

Alida did not answer, and after a moment the Grand Duchess said quietly:

"I cannot imagine what the Prince can have said to you. He told me there was a man he wanted to help, and that you might be able to assist him."

"His Royal Highness ... wanted to help ... him?"

It was difficult for Alida to speak the words.

The Grand Duchess nodded her head.

"But I thought ... I understood ... that ..."

"Have you not realised," the Grand Duchess interrupted, "that the Prince could never do anything to harm a fellow-creature? His whole life is dedicated to helping and assisting those less fortunate than himself."

Alida looked at the Grand Duchess wide-eyed as she continued:

"I thought someone would have told you already that it was I who suggested to the Emperor he should give the Serfs their emancipation."

"It was your ... idea, Ma'am?" Alida ejaculated.

"It is an ideal I have worked for secretly ever since I came to Russia," the Grand Duchess replied, "but I realised it would not be easy and that was why I sent for Vladimir to come to St. Petrsburg."

Tears were still wet on Alida's cheeks, but her eyes were fixed on the Grand Duchess's face as she continued.

"Vladimir is a Georgian, and Georgians, as you very likely know, are not Russians. Their country was joined to Russia only in this century and the last part of its territory was amalgamated with ours only eleven years ago."

She smiled.

"The Georgians are quite different in character from the Russians. They are gay, happy people, with no Tartar and no Slav blood in them. You will find, dear child, very little cruelty amongst the Georgians."

"I did ... not ... understand," Alida murmured almost beneath her breath.

"All the people who serve Vladimir—and he has great properties—are free," the Grand Duchess went on, "and that is why for two years he has been trying to persuade the Tsar to compel the Russian Noblemen to release their Serfs. He is the driving force in the Central Committee for Emancipation."

Alida put her hands to her face and wiped away her tears with the tips of her fingers.

"Shall I go . . . back, Ma'am, and . . . apologise?" she asked in a very small voice.

"I think that would be the right thing to do," the Grand Duchess replied.

Alida rose to her feet.

"I should have . . . thought before I . . . spoke," she said hesitatingly.

"That is something we all should do!" the Grand Duchess replied. "But fortunately we often forget, otherwise the world would be a much duller place."

She smiled encouragingly at Alida.

"Go and make your peace with my dear Vladimir," she said. "He will understand if you tell him that you misjudged him."

Mr. Stroyensky was still playing as Alida left the Salon. She walked very slowly through the Ante-Room she had traversed so quickly a few minutes before.

It was hard to know what to say! It would be difficult to apologise.

She realised that she had been very foolish and had acted with an impetuosity which would have brought swift retribution from her Uncle and of which even her father would have disapproved.

She opened the door of the Library, and because she was shy at the apology she must make she walked very softly into the big room.

The Prince was sitting in the armchair in front of the fire, where she had left him, and was staring at the flames. He did not hear her enter.

For a moment she stood watching him.

She realised that there was a sad, almost desperate expression on his face to which she could not put a name. Then as if instinctively he sensed her presence, rather than heard her, he looked up.

Their eyes met across the room and it seemed to Alida that something strange happened. Something unexpected and yet so magnetic that it held them both spellbound.

For a moment she could not move—she could hardly breathe—and then in a low voice that was difficult to hear she said:

"I have . . . come back . . . to apologise."

Chapter Five

The Prince rose to his feet, and very slowly, as if she was compelled to do so, Alida moved towards him.

When she reached the hearth-rug she stood still. He seemed very large, tall, and somehow overwhelming. After a second she faltered.

"I am ... sorry ... I did not ... understand."

Their eyes met and then, unexpectedly, the Prince asked:

"Who has beaten you?"

Alida felt the colour rush into her cheeks in a crimson tide, until looking away from him towards the fire she answered:

"My ... Uncle."

"How could any man beat a flower?" the Prince asked in such a low voice that she felt she had not heard him aright.

"Shall we sit down?" he suggested quietly.

He indicated with his hand the chair that Alida had occupied before, but instead she sat down on the hearth-rug, which was a white bear-skin.

Her grey skirt billowed out round her, and she turned her face away from the Prince so that he could see only her small straight nose and exquisite features silhouetted against the flames of the fire.

He seated himself in the deep-red leather armchair and sat watching her. After a silence that seemed to continue for a long time he said softly:

"Why should your Uncle have beaten you? What could you have done that was so wrong?"

"He ... hates me," Alida replied.

Without considering what she should say, she felt that she must tell the Prince the truth.

He did not question her, and yet she felt that he was waiting for her to tell him more, and after a few seconds had passed she said hesitatingly:

"Perhaps ... that is not ... true. It is not so much that my Uncle ... hates me as that he ... punishes me for something ... my father did of which he ... disapproves."

"And what was that?"

The Prince did not sound curious and yet the question was somehow a command and without thinking Alida replied:

"He ... married my ... mother, of whom my Uncle ... disapproved."

Even as she spoke she remembered that the Duke had told her not to speak of her father's marriage when she was in St. Petersburg, and now she turned towards the Prince to say with a note of fear in her voice:

"I was told not to speak of it. Please ... do not tell Mary that I have ... told you."

"Anything we say to each other here," the Prince replied, "is secret and confidential."

He paused for a moment, then added:

"The reason why I asked the Grand Duchess to bring you to this part of the Palace is that here there are no eavesdroppers."

"You mean that the Third Section of the Secret Chancellory would not be informed of anything we say here?" Alida asked.

"Exactly!" the Prince answered. "So tell me the reason for your Uncle's animosity."

"I think it is a ... mistake for me to talk about ... myself," Alida replied. "You were asking me about ... Mr. Tatkenski."

"For the moment I am more interested in you," the Prince answered, "and because you have already told me so much, you must tell me the rest, otherwise I shall feel you still do not trust me."

"But I ... do."

"I want you to trust me."

She turned her head towards the Prince. The light from the fire made her fair hair seem like a halo round her heart-shaped face with its big, worried, dark eyes.

"I hope never again," the Prince said gently, "to hear the note of fear in your voice that you revealed just now. Only someone who has suffered as you must have suffered could have spoken in such a way."

Alida made a little gesture with her hands. She bent her head so that the Prince could not see her face.

"Tell me," he said again very softly.

"My . . . mother," she replied, "was a . . . ballerina."

The words were spoken, and now that she had actually said them Alida felt a sudden panic-stricken fear that the Prince might, like her Uncle, feel that she was something almost unclean.

She felt as though he had hypnotised her into telling the truth, and if she could have taken back the words she had just spoken, she would have done so.

She waited with every muscle in her body tense, every nerve alert for a change of intonation in his voice, or perhaps a movement when he would rise to his feet and the interview would be at an end.

The Prince bent forward in his chair.

"Is there anything wrong in that?"

Alida's chin came up and she turned her eyes to his.

"Papa did not think it . . . wrong," she answered, "but to my Uncle it is something . . . disgraceful, something he considers a . . . blot upon the family . . . honour."

"Where did your mother dance?" the Prince enquired.

"In Vienna," Alida answered. "She was a member of the Imperial Corps de Ballet. Papa met her when he was posted in the British Embassy there."

The Prince gave an exclamation.

"Now I understand!" he cried unexpectedly. "Now I know what it is that has been perplexing me ever since I first saw you."

Alida had expected him to say many things, but

not this, and her eyes were wide in surprise as the Prince went on:

"Come, I have something to show you."

He put out his hand and drew her to her feet. As her fingers touched his she felt a strange little thrill run through her, almost as if it were quicksilver.

Without releasing her hand, he drew her across the big Library to where at the far end there was a huge, flat-topped desk.

There were piles of official-looking papers, an ornate gold ink-stand, and a number of white quill pens stuck into a pot of lapis lazuli.

The desk faced the room and the Prince drew Alida round it to the high-backed velvet armchair in which he sat to write.

On the desk beside the ink-pot was a large miniature in a frame set with diamonds and turquoises. Painted on ivory was the head and shoulders of an exquisitely lovely woman.

Her hair was the deep Titian red beloved by artists. She had a heart-shaped face and large, dark eyes that seemed almost purple in their depths.

The Prince picked up the picture and held it closer to Alida. The light from two large candles fell on it.

"This was my mother," he said. "Do you see anything about the picture which you recognise?"

"Recognise?" Alida asked.

She sensed that there was some strange excitement in the Prince's voice, and she had felt it in the touch of his hand on hers.

She looked again at the portrait, trying to understand what he was telling her.

Then it struck her that there was something in the shape of the eyes, the size of the pupils, and the manner in which the dark lashes stood out from the lids that was undoubtedly familiar.

"I think," she said in a low voice, "although you may think it very ... presumptuous of me, that your mother's eyes ... which are very beautiful, resemble a little those of my ... Mama."

She was afraid that the Prince might be annoyed, or perhaps even shocked, that she should compare her mother with his. Instead he said in a tone of triumph:

"They also resemble yours!"

"Mine?"

Again she felt the colour come into her cheeks because she was so astonished that he should say such a thing.

"What was your mother's name?" he enquired.

"Eisnerz," Alida replied.

The Prince put down the portrait and, pulling open one of the desk drawers, drew out a long scroll.

He put it down on the desk and, pushing aside a pen-tray, a clock, a calendar, and a letter-opener, he started to unroll it.

"This is my Family Tree," he explained. "It starts with an ancestor who was Greek, and I understand most successful in the Olympic Games. He came to Georgia as a Conqueror and remained as a King."

"A Greek!" Alida exclaimed. "Then that of course explains why you ..."

She stopped, realising that what she had been about to say was perhaps too intimate.

"Will you finish that sentence?" the Prince asked.

"Once again ... I was speaking without ... thinking."

"Which I hope you will always do with me."

Alida gave him a shy little smile.

"Then I was going to say your Greek ancestry would account for Your Highness's ... good looks."

"Thank you," he said quietly. "I have been teased about my appearance too often to find it anything but an embarrassment."

He went on unrolling the scroll until he came nearly to the bottom.

"There is a name here I want you to read," he said. "It belonged to my Great-Grandmother."

He pointed with his finger and Alida bent forward to read, and clearly inscribed on the roll she saw the name Eisnerz.

She stared at it, hardly believing the evidence of her own eyes. Then she said in a voice that trembled:

"You ... said your ... Great-Grandmother?"

"I have always been told my mother was very like her," the Prince replied. "Family characteristics are handed down from generation to generation. I think that you and I are undoubtedly connected, if not actually cousins."

"Could that really be true?" Alida asked. "I have always understood that my Great-Grandfather was impoverished in Napoleon's wars, and my Grandfather was killed fighting with the Austrian Army. When he died, he had no money to leave his wife, which was why my mother became a . . . ballerina."

She found that it was difficult to say the word which had been drilled into her so long as a shame and disgrace.

"So your mother was the bread-winner for the family," the Prince said quietly.

"She often told me how poor they were. How her younger brothers and sisters went hungry, and her mother, growing thinner and thinner, would sit up night after night trying to earn a little money by sewing."

"It happened to a great number of Austrian families," the Prince said. "But however poor they might be, they were always proud, always distinguished, always noble."

Alida felt the tears come into her eyes, and because she did not wish the Prince to see them she bent lower over the scroll, as if to be quite certain that she had read the name of his Great-Grandmother correctly.

"In Russia," the Prince said, "there is a great respect for those who have a talent either for music or for the Ballet. There is one house where your mother, if she were alive, would always be welcome, and that is this one."

"Thank you for saying that," Alida answered. "But please do not tell the Grand Duchess what I have told you. She might mention it to Mary, and if the Duke learnt that I had disobeyed him he would be very angry."

"You mean he would beat you?" the Prince asked. "You told me the Russians were cruel, but I have no words to express what I feel about a man who could hurt or humiliate something as small and exquisite as you."

"My Uncle thinks that anyone who appears on a stage of any sort must be ... immoral," Alida said. "But to me, my mother was everything that was pure and beautiful."

She drew in her breath before she added:

"It is hard to hear her defamed, to listen to her being accused of behaviour that would have been utterly foreign to her nature."

"Forget it for the moment," the Prince said. "Whatever you have been made to suffer, it cannot go on forever. You will marry, and then you will escape from your Uncle's guardianship."

There was silence.

"I can never ... marry," Alida answered in a low voice.

"What do you mean?" the Prince enquired.

"My Uncle told me before I came to Russia that he would never give his consent to my ... marriage. He said that he would not inflict me upon ... any man because of the ... bad blood which runs in my veins."

"And now you know that that blood is not bad!" the Prince exclaimed. "It is the same blood that runs in my veins—the blood of a family deeply respected and admired in Austria."

"Is that ... really the ... truth?" Alida asked pathetically.

"I swear to you it is true," the Prince replied. "Tomorrow I shall write to Vienna, to my mother's family, asking them for documents which will prove exactly how close our relationship is. You will learn about our family and will realise that there is a great deal in our ancestry of which we both can be justly proud."

Alida clasped her hands together. There was a sudden light in her eyes that made them shine like stars.

"If you only ... knew," she whispered, "what it means to ... hear you say ... that."

She looked up at the Prince and for a moment neither of them could move.

Once again they were held by a magic spell and it seemed to Alida that they were speaking to each other without words, that they were both vibrantly aware of things which they dared not express.

Then, like the thrust of a dagger in her breast, she remembered Mary! Her cousin whom the Prince was to marry! Her eyes fluttered and dropped before his.

She half-turned away from him as he said, words seeming to be forced from his lips:

"We must talk about this again. I will search amongst all the books I have with me. And it should not take long to receive a reply from Vienna. In the meantime we have another matter to discuss."

"Mr. Tatkenski?"

"Exactly!" the Prince agreed. "Let us go back to the fire-side, and I want you to tell me what happened when you met him on the English Steamer on the way to Kiel."

Alida returned to the hearth-rug and sat down on the white bear-skin as she had done before.

Quietly she explained what had happened and what Mr. Tatkenski had said to her in the Saloon on the *Maid of Hull.* How Count Ivan had seen him kissing her hand, and how from that moment he had disappeared.

"I destroyed his note," she said, "and when Count Ivan asked me when we embarked on the *Ischora* where he had said he was going, I told him Stockholm."

The Prince had listened intently to every word and now he said:

"I am quite certain that Mr. Tatkenski will come to St. Petersburg, as he intended, to try to find his mother."

"Do you know where she is?" Alida asked.

"I have a shrewd idea," the Prince answered, "and one of my most trusted men is making enquiries. But it will not be safe for Tatkenski to stay here. Nor do I think he would wish to do so."

"How can the Police arrest him when he carries a British Passport?" Alida asked.

"They will not arrest him," the Prince explained.

"He will merely be taken somewhere for questioning, and there might be a—regrettable accident."

"Can such things really happen?" Alida asked.

"Unfortunately we are in the middle of a political crisis," the Prince replied. "Those who are ardently, almost fanatically, opposed to the emancipation of the Serfs are making it their business to see that there is no disturbance of any sort amongst the Russian people."

"But Mr. Tatkenski only wants to get his mother out of Russia," Alida protested.

"As you know only too well, the sins of the fathers are visited upon the children," the Prince replied. "Tatkenski's father was a revolutionary."

"And he died in Siberia," Alida said.

"The trouble he caused has not been forgotten," the Prince told her. "Tatkenski will be a marked man from the moment he sets foot on Russian soil. Whatever his Citizenship may be officially, it will not save him."

"But you will do your . . . best?" Alida pleaded.

"I have a plan," the Prince replied, "but it all depends on you."

"On . . . me?" Alida asked in surprise.

"Do you realise that you and Count Ivan are the only people here who know what Mr. Tatkenski looks like?"

"Count Ivan!" Alida merely said the words, and yet the tone of her voice revealed all too clearly her dislike for the Count.

"What can we do?" she went on. "How can we warn Mr. Tatkenski?"

"What I would like you to do, if you are brave enough," the Prince answered, "is to identify him when he arrives in St. Petersburg."

"Have you any idea when that will be?" Alida asked.

"Ships from Kiel dock only once a week," the Prince answered, "and the reason why I had to speak to you tonight is that there is a ship arriving at seven o'clock tomorrow morning."

"And you think Mr. Tatkenski will be on it?"

"There is every possibility that he will come on this particular ship, unless he has really gone to Stockholm."

"I am quite certain he had no intention of going there," Alida said. "He only wanted me to say that because Count Ivan had been making enquiries about him."

"I thought the same, and I am sure too that, realising that Count Ivan might make things difficult for him, he will not arrive under his own name or carry a British Passport," the Prince said.

Alida looked at him in surprise, and the Prince went on:

"Mr. Tatkenski would not be his father's son unless he knew of organisations in Kiel and elsewhere which are actively opposing the Regimes in all monarchical countries. Such organisations can always provide false Passports."

"And perhaps a disguise?" Alida asked.

"There is no reason for Tatkenski to be disguised so long as neither you nor Count Ivan are waiting on the Quay when the *Bosporos* arrives tomorrow morning."

"You want me to be there?" Alida asked

"A piece of luggage will have been left behind at Kiel," the Prince answered. "It is a round-topped black-leather bag, small enough to have been overlooked. The *Bosporos* will bring it to St. Petersburg and it will be addressed to you personally."

"So I go to the Quay to claim it," Alida said.

"Exactly!" the Prince agreed. "And you will be accompanied by one of the Grand Duchess's trusted maids who knows nothing of this matter."

"I understand," Alida said.

"Before you go up the gang-plank and onto the ship to see if your baggage is waiting for you, as it will be, in the Purser's Office you will wait as the passengers disembark," the Prince went on. "If you see Mr. Tatkenski, you will not speak to him. You will make no gesture of recognition whatsoever, but as he passes you you will accidentally drop your reticule."

"I understand," Alida said, again in a low voice.

She suddenly felt afraid. Suppose she had forgotten what Mr. Tatkenski looked like? Suppose she missed him in the crowd? How terrible if he was taken for questioning because she was forgetful!

As if he read her thoughts, the Prince said quietly:

"Do not be afraid. Memory is a strange thing. Even though we do not realise it, every face we meet is engraved on our minds, and if you see Tatkenski, even though he may be disguised, you will know he is the man for whom you are looking."

"Are you sure of that?" Alida asked.

"I am quite sure," he answered consolingly. "But, whatever happens, you will have done your best."

"And suppose he does not arrive tomorrow?"

"Then we have to wait a week, but I have the feeling he will be in a hurry to find his mother."

"Yes, I am sure he will be. He was so longing to see her," Alida said.

The Prince looked thoughtful.

"I think for nearly every man his mother is someone very special. She holds a place in his heart that can later be filled only by his wife."

There was something in the way the Prince spoke, something in the look in his eyes, that made Alida feel shy.

She rose to her feet.

"Perhaps I ought to go now," she said. "The Grand Duchess will think it strange that I have been here so long."

"One day perhaps we shall be able to tell her what we have discovered about each other," the Prince said.

"I think Her Royal Highness would believe it," Alida answered, "but my Uncle would dismiss it as irrelevant. He will still continue to hate the thought of my mother, and to . . . punish me."

"Try to forget him while you are here," the Prince urged. "I want you to enjoy yourself. I want you to bloom like the little orchid which you resemble. I wanted to tell you—many new buds have burst into flower only today."

Alida smiled.

"I am glad. It is the loveliest flower I have ever

seen. I am so flattered that you should think that I in any way resemble it."

She looked up at the Prince, then looked away quickly. She did not dare face the expression in his eyes. She could not formulate even in her own mind what it might mean.

"I must ... go," she said again shyly, and moved towards the door.

She did not wish to leave.

She wanted to stay in front of the fire and talk to the Prince, to hear his deep voice, to see his handsome face by the flicker of the flames and the soft lights of the great candles.

Because she wanted so much to be with him, she knew she must go.

He followed her across the room and opened the door into the Ante-Room.

"I am ashamed," he said, "to involve you in this. The cruelty and the foulness of life is something which should never encroach upon you."

"But I want to help people like Mr. Tatkenski," Alida answered. "And if I can help, even in a little way, I shall be proud, terribly proud."

"That is how I feel when I have been able to assist somebody or to save a life," the Prince said.

As he spoke he took Alida's small hand in his and lifted it to his lips. She felt the touch of his mouth on her skin, and something strange and exciting moved within her.

Something seemed for a moment to flicker into life like a little flame. Then he released her hand and she hurried across the Ante-Room and into the Salon.

The Grand Duchess was waiting there alone.

"You have been a long time, my children," she said. "Mr. Stroyensky was so tired that I sent him to bed. He is not strong, and he is working until the early hours of the morning on an Opera which I intend to send, as soon as it is completed, to Paris."

Alida felt that the Grand Duchess was talking as if to bridge any awkwardness that might have arisen in so unconventional a situation.

"Come along, child," she said to Alida before either

she or the Prince could speak, "it is time you had
your beauty sleep. After all, there is my Ball tomorrow night."

Alida was just going to say that she could not come
to the Ball, but she realised that it would sound too
obviously as if she were asking the Grand Duchess to
give her a gown.

"It sounds very gay and exciting, Ma'am," she said
instead.

Their little sledges were waiting for them in the circular Hall.

The Prince helped the Grand Duchess into hers
and when he turned to Alida she was already seated
against the satin cushions.

"Good night, Vladimir," the Grand Duchess said. "I
am so glad you enjoyed Mr. Stroyensky's music."

"It was everything that I had expected," the Prince
said. "I hope we can persuade him to play for us
again another time."

"I am sure we can," the Grand Duchess replied.

The footmen pushed the sledges through the big
mahogany doors.

Alida longed to look back, to have a last glance at
the Prince. Though she forced herself to look straight
ahead, she was thinking of him as they moved along
the corridors.

She wondered how for even one moment she could
have suspected that he was anything but kind and
understanding.

There was something in his face that was so trustworthy, something in the expression in his eyes that
should have told her from the beginning that he was
incapable of cruelty.

He was in fact the very opposite of Count Ivan and
his father.

Alida felt herself shivering a little as she thought of
the General's tyranny over the young Cadets and
Count Ivan's relentless pursuit of Mr. Tatkenski.

'I must remember what he looked like—I must save
him!' she told herself.

But because she was frightened she found that her
memory of his face was just a blank.

She could recall what he had said, the pain in his voice when he spoke of the horrors perpetrated on the Hebrew children, and the sudden softness that had been there when he spoke of his mother.

'I sometimes think that I have suffered,' Alida said to herself, 'but it is nothing to what these people have endured. I must be brave. I must not let myself feel so humiliated when Uncle Septumus beats me. I must try not to scream.'

But she knew despairingly that she had not enough courage to stand up to her Uncle.

She accused herself of being physically a coward, when every nerve in her small body shrank from the beatings he would inflict on her.

Moreover, she felt sure that when she returned home, after Mary was married, his persecution would be even more violent than it had been before.

'Oh, God, how can I bear it?' she asked herself in the darkness of her bed-room.

She turned out the light but could not sleep. She found herself going over and over again what the Prince had said.

'If only I could tell Mama,' she thought, 'that her relative is one of the most important men in Russia! If only she could know there are people in the world who respect her and are not ashamed because she danced for her living.'

It was hard to think of the insults which her mother had endured all her life from the Shenleys and their bigoted attitude towards anyone who appeared on the stage.

Alida was sure that her father had never regretted the fact that he was forced to leave the Diplomatic Service, but it must have been in many ways hurtful for him to realise that his brother disapproved so strongly of his wife.

All the time they lived in Paris not one single Shenley relative had ever come to call on them.

Yet never, Alida told herself, had two people been as happy as her father and mother had been together.

They had very little money—only a small annuity that an Aunt had settled on her father on her death, and which had ceased when he died. But they had been happy.

Looking back, their house, small though it had been and in an unfashionable part of Paris, had always seemed full of light and sunshine.

They had been surrounded by friends—friends who had talent, friends with intelligence, with ideas, with ideals, Men of Letters, artists, scholars, and politicians.

'Rather the same sort of people,' Alida thought now, 'as the Grand Duchess entertains at the Palace. The Intelligentsia are the same all the world over.'

Then she realised that, whilst once again she was amongst people who were interesting, were exciting to listen to, and whom she admired, it was only a brief respite from the gloom and the misery that awaited her at the Castle.

As soon as Mary was married, Alida was to go home "by the cheapest and quickest route," and must leave behind everything in this strange new world that seemed at the moment so entrancing and so attractive.

'And one person seems more attractive than all the others!' a voice whispered inside her.

'He belongs to Mary!' her conscience told her severely.

Hiding her face in the pillow, she fought against the tears which unaccountably had come into her eyes.

The following morning Alida arrived back at the Palace in a sleigh, accompanied by a quiet and respectful attendant of the Grand Duchess.

It was barely eight o'clock because the ship had docked on time.

Their business over, they had swept back through almost empty streets, the sledge gliding with a strange rhythmic movement over the first fall of snow which had occurred the night before.

Alida had been asleep when there had come a quiet knock at the door, and a maid had entered to draw back the curtains to show a grey, overcast sky.

She had required lights by which to dress, and she

had hurried, knowing that whatever happened she must not awaken Mary or the Countess, sleeping in the adjoining rooms.

A flunkey was waiting to escort her down a different staircase from the one they habitually used.

In a small Hall, where there was a sidedoor to the Palace, an elderly woman was waiting, wrapped in a thick cloak and wearing a dark, untrimmed bonnet which declared her to be a senior servant.

She curtseyed and followed Alida outside.

"Snow!" Alida exclaimed. "I knew it would be here soon, but even so, surely it is early?"

"We expect Winter, *Ma'm'selle*, from the first of October," the woman replied in French, "and now there will be no more carriages until the Spring."

"Instead we will be in sledges," Alida cried. "How exciting!"

The one which was waiting for her was large, elaborate, and very luxurious, pulled by four well-matched horses.

But in the streets Alida saw smaller ones with high-trotting horses which seemed to move at a much faster speed.

The sledge was very comfortable. Alida was covered with a thick fur rug, and as she had left the Palace she was handed a large fur muff in which to place her hands.

By the time they reached the Quay-side, which was some distance away, the sun was struggling through the clouds and Alida thought that the spires, the domes, and the great Palaces covered in snow were the most beautiful sight she had ever seen.

It had been a heavy fall and everything was white.

She thought that St. Petersburg looked like fairyland, until she remembered that under the surface there was cruelty and terror, fear and misery.

The Quay looked dingy in the early morning, but there was a great deal of activity, and for the first time since she had come to St. Petersburg Alida had time to notice the people.

The men were as a whole finely built, tall and rather wild-looking.

They were warmly clothed, wearing great boots and enfolding coats of thick sheep-skin, which seemed to blend with their long beards and tangled hair.

There were few women, but those there were squat and ugly and so muffled up that Alida thought that most of them, with only the tips of their noses showing through a thick shawl of fur hood, looked like fat cocoons.

The sledge had been waiting for only a few minutes on the Quay when there was the sound of hooting and a Steamer appeared round the bend of the river.

"That will be the *Bosporos, Ma'm'selle,*" Alida's companion said.

Alida could not help thinking that it did not look a very impressive vessel and certainly compared unfavourably with the English Steamer which had carried them from Harwich to Kiel.

The moment the Steamer began to dock, an enormous crowd of people seemed to appear from nowhere. They stood on the Quay-side shouting to their friends who were standing on dock.

There was also a large number of porters who waited apathetically, as if they did not expect to earn much money at that hour of the morning.

Nevertheless, despite the shabby appearance of the ship, it appeared to be crowded. There were many strong young peasants on board clad in sheep-skin coats and thick, high boots.

There were Officers of rank, as varied in their features as in their uniforms. There were Tradesmen with flowing beards and long-skirted Kaftans.

There was also a large number of indescribable persons, dark and stern-looking with no-one to meet them and from their expressions not particularly elated at having reached their destination.

As soon as the gang-plank was down, Alida descended from the sleigh, followed by her companion.

She made no explanation as to why she appeared in no hurry to board the ship, and merely proceeded to stand on one side as the passengers filed onto the Quay, most of them carrying their baggage.

The First-Class passengers were ushered off first and it was obvious to Alida that Mr. Tatkenski was not amongst them. Somehow, she had not expected him to be.

If he was going to change his identity, she was quite certain that he would not travel First Class. That would be to invite comment.

Following the First-Class passengers—and there were not many of them—there came a number of the more respectable Tradesmen and professional men, neatly dressed with well-combed beards, and wearing expensive fur hats on their heads.

When they were ashore, there came the Steerage passengers. Women carrying babies in their arms, old men lugging enormous packages which seemed too heavy for them.

There were children looking tired, or being annoyingly obstreperous, and finally a number of men who Alida knew from their clothing were Serfs.

Many of these were undersized. Others were large and seemed almost ashamed of their height, and then there came a man who carried a bale on his shoulder.

Alida had only one quick glance at his face but, as the Prince had expected, she recognised him immediately.

Mr. Tatkenski was unshaven, and his dress was deliberately untidy and ragged, but Alida would have known him anywhere.

He reached the end of the gang-plank and as he did so she dropped her reticule. She gave a little exclamation and bending her head to look down on the ground deliberately avoided looking Mr. Tatkenski in the face.

"How stupid of me!" she exclaimed.

"*Merci, merci bien,*" she added to her companion, who picked up the little grey bag and gave it back into her hand.

By the time she raised her head Mr. Tatkenski was some way down the Quay. Without appearing to look after him, Alida saw a man come towards him and take him by the arm.

They were talking together as they moved away to

where a sleigh was waiting. It was an unpainted, cheap-looking sleigh drawn by one horse.

Alida knew without being told that the man who had met Mr. Tatkenski was the Prince's man and would direct him to his mother.

With a little sigh of thankfulness she realised that her task was done, and then remembered almost with a start that she still had to go on board to retrieve the luggage which was to be the explanation for her leaving the Palace so early.

It took Alida a little time to discover the box which was just inside the Purser's Office.

She guessed that it had been taken on board by the Pilot ship which had brought the Steamer into port.

As there was no-one to whom she could speak of such ideas, she merely thanked the purser for supplying her with the lost luggage and her companion tipped the porter, who carried it to the sleigh.

They drove home at a great speed.

Alida was unable to have much conversation with the woman who accompanied her, since the cold wind seemed to whip away the words from her lips.

Alida found it easier to hold her muff over her mouth so that only her eyes looked round at the grandeur, magnificence, and beauty of the City.

She was taken upstairs to her room in the Palace by the same staircase by which she had left it.

She looked at her clock and realised that Mary would still not be awake—in fact no-one would know where she had been or what she had done.

She thought to herself that it all seemed rather like a dream—something that did not happen to ordinary people. But she was sure now that with the Prince's assistance Mr. Tatkenski would find his mother and, having found her, they would both be helped out of the country.

'At least one person will be free!' Alida thought.

Despite every resolution to the contrary, she could not help thinking that she herself could never be free, but must remain a captive for life.

Chapter Six

His Imperial Majesty, Emperor Alexander II, Tsar of all the Russians, was reviewing his Troops.

He looked extremely impressive on horseback, wearing a white tunic festooned in decorations, while the horse-cloth that covered his mount was of red, embroidered with the Imperial Coat of Arms.

In front of him marched the crack Regiment of the *Chevaliers Gardes* and the *Gardes à 'Cheval*. After them came the Hussars, commanded by the Heritier, the Lancers, Grenadiers, and Cossacks.

Every soldier looked exactly the same as the soldier next to him, while every horse of a Regiment was the same size, colour, and shape.

In the Barracks of the First Corps of Cadets, Alida with Mary and the Countess sat at one window in the General's private room, while the other three windows were occupied by distinguished notabilities.

The Barracks on the Wassili Ostow measured, Alida was told, a quarter of an English mile square, while the length of its rooms and uninhabited places added up to nearly seven miles. It housed over three thousand Cadets.

The Parade was awe-inspiring in its size—there must have been over ten thousand men taking part—but Alida's eyes were attracted rather to the magnificent buildings stretching towards the Neva, their coloured domes and spires bright against the grey sky.

It was fantastic, a City which had been the dream-child of its founder, Peter the Great.

The Countess rose to speak to some acquaintances

who had just entered the room, and Alida, feeling that perhaps her silence showed a lack of enthusiasm, said to Mary:

"I have never seen such a big Parade!"

Her cousin did not answer and after a moment, because she wanted to know the answer, Alida asked:

"Is the Prince with the Emperor's entourage? I cannot see him."

"No," Mary replied, "he is with the Committee for the Emancipation of the Serfs, and doing, Count Ivan tells me, incredible harm."

Her voice was sharp as she went on:

"Ivan says that if the Prince has his way, the whole structure of Russian society will crumble into the dust and thousands of Noblemen will be ruined."

"I am sure His Highness has taken that into consideration," Alida murmured.

"Ivan thinks," Mary continued as if she has not heard, "that someday someone will murder the Prince. In fact, Ivan swears that if he has the chance he himself will push His Highness under the ice and leave him there until he drowns."

Alida looked at Mary incredulously.

"How can you say such things about the man you are to marry?" she asked.

"Do you imagine I wish to marry a pauper, or to live in a country where there is no-one to serve us?"

"We do not have Serfs in England, yet a number of people contrive to be very comfortable," Alida replied.

"That is different!" Mary snapped. "Are you so stupid that you do not understand that a man's wealth here depends on the number of Serfs he owns?

"The Benkendorf family would be crippled without the thousands of 'souls' which have been theirs for generations. You can imagine the feelings of Count Sheremctief, who possesses himself a hundred fifty thousand male Serfs."

Alida bit back the words of argument which came to her lips, and Mary said, almost as if she consoled herself:

"However, the Prince will not be successful. He may think he has the sympathy of the Tsar, he may continue to use his influence with a few Noblemen of little consequence. But the great land-owners are against him and they will defeat him! If not, something else will have to be done, something drastic and decisive!"

"Are you really suggesting that His Highness might be murdered?" Alida asked with a note of horror in her voice.

"Ivan says that he is hated to such an extent by some members of the Committee that he is only surprised that this has not happened already."

There was a silence and then Mary added with a little smile:

"Of course, the Count is prejudiced. After all, he is very jealous that I am to be the Prince's bride."

Alida drew in her breath.

"When is the announcement to be . . . made?"

"I do not know," Mary replied. "The Prince has not mentioned it to me yet and the Grand Duchess is rather vague. But I am in no hurry. Anyway, it will not be at the Ball tonight, and certainly not tomorrow night."

She gave a little laugh.

"What is happening tomorrow night?" Alida asked.

"Did I not tell you?" Mary laughed. "Ivan is giving a Ball at the Benkendorf Palace, and of course, although he cannot say so, it is for me."

"What about his wife?" Alida asked. "Will she be there?"

Mary shook her head.

"I am glad to say that she is away from home, visiting her family in Moscow. I cannot tell you how much I am looking forward to seeing Ivan's Palace—or what will be his when the General dies."

"Where in St. Petersburg is it?" Alida enquired.

"It is not in the City, but outside," Mary answered. "Ivan's ancestor was furious at being made to build a home in St. Petersburg, as were all the other Nobles who were commanded to do so by Peter the Great."

She smiled as she continued:

"So, to show his independence, the Count Benkendorf of the day built his Palace two miles outside the Capital. I believe it is extremely impressive and very luxurious."

Alida said nothing.

When Mary spoke of Count Ivan and his Palace there was a kind of proprietary note in her voice which was both wrong and dangerous.

Publicly they could mean nothing to each other, and Alida was certain that already St. Petersburg society must be talking of their quite obvious mutual infatuation.

They would have been blind not to notice the manner in which Count Ivan singled out Mary for his attentions.

He had chosen the best viewpoint of the Parade. Alida felt that it must have been noted and commented upon by the other ladies in the room.

Now the Countess returned to her seat as below them the Regiment of Cossacks in scarlet and blue passed the Emperor. Riding superbly, each man held his long, naked lance vertical, the pointed shafts rising like a red forest over the ranks.

"I am glad to have seen the Parade," the Countess said as she seated herself. "I have been away from St. Petersburg for so long that I had forgotten how magnificent it is."

"The Grand Duchess said before we left the Palace," Alida remarked, "that you were leaving today, Ma'am. Is that true?"

"I am going to Moscow to meet my husband," the Countess replied.

"Will it be a difficult journey with so much snow?" Alida enquired.

"It would have been, a few years back," the Countess replied. "But now there is a comfortable train to carry me there."

She smiled reminiscently as she said:

"Tsar Nicholas disliked railways and opposed their being built. In the short time the present Emperor has been on the throne, he has increased the construction of railways fantastically."

"It must have been very tiring to go all the way by sleigh," Alida said.

"It was indeed," the Countess replied, "and not only tiring, but dangerous."

"From the wolves?" Alida asked.

The Countess smiled.

"From the wolves and the roads! The roads were appallingly rough, and one was in danger of being overturned or bogged down every mile of the journey. That of course gave the wolves their opportunity."

"Do they really kill travellers?" Alida asked.

The Countess laughed.

"Everybody in Russia has a wolf- or a bear-tale," she answered. "They vary according to who relates them! The favourite is the one about the lady who saw a bear in her garden and threw at it the novel she was reading, which was so immoral that the bear fled in horror!"

Alida laughed.

"But the wolves can be dangerous to travellers," the Countess went on more seriously, "especially when they hunt in packs. St. Petersburg is the one Capital in the world where a man can enjoy the sport of wolf- or bear-hunting by just stepping outside the City boundries."

"That sounds strange," Alida smiled.

"It is really much the same as in England, where foxes and deer are hunted," the Countess explained. "It is very important that such savage beasts should be kept under control.

"The last time I was in St. Petersburg in the Winter a whole pack prowled into the gardens of the Imperial Palace in search of food."

"I hope that I never see a wolf!" Alida cried. "They sound terrifying!"

"They are," the Countess agreed. "That is why you can imagine I am glad to be travelling to Moscow by train."

The last of the Cossack Regiments was riding past the Emperor. As Alida bent forward to watch them, admiring their fine carriage and noting that they rode with very short stirrups, she realised that Count Ivan was beside Mary and whispering in her ear.

The Countess was looking out the window and Mary turned to say to Alida in a low voice:

"Ivan is taking me to see a man flogged. If the General returns after the Parade, keep him interested until we return."

Alida looked at her cousin with an expression of horror in her eyes. She wanted to expostulate! She wanted to beg her to watch nothing so beastly and degrading.

But Mary, without waiting for an answer, had risen from her chair. With a little flurry of her wide skirt and a swing to her crinoline, she moved with Count Ivan across the long room and out through the door.

It all happened so swiftly that Alida was not ready with an answer when the Countess turned from the window to ask in surprise:

"Where has Lady Mary gone?"

"I think Count Ivan had ... something to ... show her," Alida replied.

"I am sure he had," the Countess said dryly, and added in a kind voice:

"Do not look so worried, my dear. You will find as you grow older that people must do what they wish to do, and nothing we can say will stop them."

"I do not wish Mary to do anything that is wrong or might damage her reputation," Alida replied.

The Countess had been so kind to her ever since they had left England that she felt it was no indiscretion to speak so plainly.

"Count Ivan is a very experienced flirt," the Countess said slowly. "He is behaving, as we both know, extremely reprehensibly, but I do not think the Grand Duchess is aware of the liaison, or whatever it may be. We can only hope that when your cousin's engagement is announced, she will behave in a more circumspect manner."

"I would ... like you, Ma'am, to speak to Mary about it," Alida said hesitatingly, "before you leave."

The Countess shook her head.

"No, my dear, my mission is at its end. I was told

to chaperon you both from England. Now I am off-duty, so to speak!" She paused.

"At the same time, I only hope that your cousin will realise that she is to be married to a man who is respected and admired not only in Russia, but in many parts of Europe."

"I am sure she will realise . . . it in time," Alida said, and wondered why her own voice sounded so flat, with something like a note of despair in it.

Below, on the Parade-ground, the Emperor, followed by his entourage of Noblemen, Ambassadors, and Aides-de-Camp, took this leave of the General and rode away.

Seeing the General ride back towards the Palace, Alida thought with a sense of panic that he would obviously come at once to his private room to greet his guests who had been watching the Parade.

To her consternation, she realised that, now that the Parade was over, they too were collecting their wraps in preparation for making their departure.

They all seemed to be intimate with the Countess and were wishing her *bon voyage* and making their farewells, so Alida stood alone.

As the General entered through the door he came directly towards her.

He was certainly impressive in his uniform. His riding-boots shone so brightly that they seemed almost to act as mirrors, while his medals and decorations almost covered the left part of his red tunic.

"What did you think of my Troops, Miss Shenley?" he asked Alida. "Have you ever seen a more magnificent or impressive collection of men?"

"Never, General," Alida answered.

"That is the result of rigorous training," the General said. "There was only one mistake in the whole Parade, and that was unfortunately committed by one of my own Cadets. He will be punished for it—make no mistake about that—and punished severely!"

"Are such punishments really . . . necessary?"

"There are people with soft hearts and sloppy minds," the General replied, "who think the branding, flogging, and *spitzruthen*—or, as you would say, flogging through the ranks—are out-of-date. But I do not agree!"

There was almost a gloating note in his voice as if he enjoyed the thought of such punishments.

Alida felt as if her voice had died in her throat, yet because she felt she must say something she managed to ask:

"For how long must an ordinary ... soldier remain in the Army?"

"Twenty-five years," the General answered.

Alida looked at him, wondering if she could have heard aright.

"Yes, twenty-five years," he repeated. "His service ends when he is forty-six."

"That is a life-time!" Alida exclaimed.

"That is what it is meant to be," the General replied. "A life-time of service to his Imperial Majesty and to his country."

"But what happens to his family?"

"After three years his wife is permitted to marry again," the General said indifferently, and as if he was not interested in the subject he added:

"I would like to show you some of the trophies that my own Regiment have won and those which have been achieved by my Cadets."

He looked round the room, which was rapidly emptying, and said to a lady who had come up to congratulate him on the Parade:

"Will you not join us, Princess? I am going to show our English visitor the trophies of the Regiment."

"How kind of you, General, but I have seen them before," the Princess answered. "We really must go or we shall be late for luncheon."

"Perhaps we should be leaving too," Alida said quickly.

She looked towards the Countess, who was detaching herself somewhat reluctantly from some friends near the door.

Then with a sense of deep relief she saw Mary, accompanied by Count Ivan, return to the room by another entrance.

"Perhaps I could see your trophies another day,

General," she said. "I am sure that the Grand Duchess will be expecting us."

Her cousin and the Countess confirmed that they should now go, and yet it seemed to Alida a long time before they could complete their farewells and leave the Barracks.

Seated beside Mary in the sleigh, covered with the fine, thick fur rug which the Grand Duchess had provided for her guests, Alida felt that there was a sense of excitement about her cousin and a glitter in her eyes which seemed vaguely familiar.

Then she realised that it was the way the Duke looked after he had beaten her!

'They both are sadists!' she thought with a sick horror.

Alida saw that Mary was holding in her hand a long, thick stick.

Her eyes rested on it, and Mary said with a sly smile:

"A souvenir! I thought it would be interesting to possess one."

"You . . . mean it is that . . . stick," Alida said in horror, "which has . . ."

She could not find the words to say any more. She could only turn her face away to look blindly at the buildings they were passing and feel a physical nausea.

Back at the Michailow Palace, they were, as Alida had expected, late for luncheon. But the Grand Duchess merely replied to their apologies:

"Parades are alway unpredictable. My brother, the last Tsar, prolonged them so that we were often famished by the time we returned home."

Alida and Mary left their wraps in their rooms and ran down the corridors to the Grand Duchess's private apartments.

'Palaces are too big!' Alida thought. 'It takes too long to move from one place to another.'

The Prince, who arrived a few minutes after them, made the same excuse.

"I have been trying to estimate," he said to the Grand Duchess, as he kissed her hand, "how much time is expended in travelling from my apartments to yours. I have a feeling there should be a quicker and shorter way of reaching each other."

"Then you will have to discover it," the Grand Duchess said fondly. "I often said that the Palace is over-large but no-one will listen to me."

Luncheon was served not in the big Banqueting-Hall, which Alida guessed was being prepared for the Ball that evening, but in the Grand Duchess's small private Dining-Room, which was part of her personal apartments.

It was a lovely oval room with a matchless mother-of-pearl floor and white-and-gold panelling on which hung gay French pictures by Watteau and Boucher.

The very room itself had an exuberant atmosphere about it, and Alida, despite the intensity of her feelings during the morning, found herself laughing and trying to forget all the things that had perturbed her.

Then unexpectedly the Grand Duchess said:

"I am looking forward to presenting two such lovely English girls to my Russian friends. I hope you both have gorgeous gowns with which to dazzle the very fashion-conscious Russian socialites who, as I well know, are extremely critical."

"I am sure my gown will not disappoint you, Ma'am," Mary replied with a self-confident smile.

"And is yours also pretty?" the Grand Duchess enquired, looking at Alida. "I shall enjoy seeing you in white, for you have worn nothing but grey ever since you came here."

There was a moment's silence and then with the blood rising in her cheeks, Alida stammered:

"I ... I ... I am afraid ... I have nothing but ... grey ..."

"My mother," Mary interposed, "considers grey suitable for Alida in her position in life. She has no white gown, so she will not be attending at the Ball tonight."

"Not be attending my Ball?" the Grand Duchess exclaimed.

There was an almost imperceptible pause before the Prince said:

"I see that the Grand Duchess has not had time to tell our honoured guests of the excellent idea Her Royal Highness had a few days ago."

"What idea was that, Vladimir?" the Grand Duchess enquired.

"You suggested, Ma'am," the Prince answered, looking her straight in the eye, "that it would give a charming and original touch to your Ball if our English visitors should personify the loveliness of the English flowers."

The Prince's voice became impressive as he continued:

"Your Royal Highness suggested that Lady Mary, who after all is the perfect example of an English rose, should symbolise that beautiful flower, and I have in fact grown some white roses in the Conservatory which can be attached to her gown at the last moment!"

He smiled and added:

"They are only just in bud and so should retain their freshness until the Ball is over."

There was an amused twist on the Grand Duchess's lips and a twinkle in her eyes as she said:

"But of course, Vladimir! How very foolish of me to have forgotten what we arranged. And what flower is Alida to represent?"

"I had thought my white star orchids were particularly suitable," the Prince answered.

"Orchids!" Mary remarked shrilly. "That is hardly an English flower, and I should not consider it in any way suitable for Alida, who, to say the least of it, could hardly be called exotic."

There was something so scathing and contemptuous in her tone that it made the blood flow once again into Alida's cheeks.

She was well aware of what the Prince was doing, and while she longed to protest and tell him that it was not important whether she came to the Ball, she was deeply touched by his thought for her.

The Prince's eyes were on Mary as he said quietly:

"I had of course thought that white English violets would have been the most obvious choice for your cousin. Their scent is in my opinion of the loveliest in the world, but unfortunately, amongst all the flowers we have grown in the Conservatory, we have no white violets. I am therefore offering, as you will appreciate, what I have available."

"I am sure it is quite unnecessary for you to take so much trouble over Alida," Mary said.

"Like yourself, she is a guest of Russia," the Prince answered, with just a faint shadow of rebuke in his voice.

"Let us hope she is grateful for such solicitude, which she certainly does not get at home," Mary said spitefully.

As if she was afraid that the Prince might make some sharp retort, the Grand Duchess rose to her feet.

"I have already ordered gowns as a background for the roses and orchids," she said, "and now there are a great many things I must see to because, like every good Hostess, I want my Ball to be a success.

"What I would suggest, Vladimir, is that after they have said good-bye to the Countess, who is now to our regret leaving us, you take Mary and Alida up to the top of the Palace to see the view."

"Count Ivan is calling to show me some of the sights of St. Petersburg," Mary remarked. "His . . . cousin will chaperon me."

Alida knew that Mary was lying and that no-one would chaperon her, but the Grand Duchess merely remarked:

"I am sure the Count would also like to see the view before you leave on your drive."

The Count must have had a very quick luncheon, Alida decided, for when they reached the Grand Duchess's Sitting-Room he was already waiting for them.

They said good-bye to the Countess, and it was with deep regret that Alida realised it was unlikely she would ever meet her again.

"It is difficult for me to thank you, Ma'am, for all your kindness to me," she said in a low voice.

To her surprise the Countess kissed her cheek.

"I shall think of you, little Alida," she said, "and pray that you will find happiness."

Then, before Alida could reply, she said her farewells to the Grand Duchess, and the Prince and Count Ivan escorted Mary and Alida up the stairway that led to the top floor.

They entered a room built under the pointed elevation which decorated the front of the Palace. The Prince explained that it had been designed for the special purpose of furnishing a look-out.

From it they could admire the vastness of the Great Okhta which stretched as far as the eye could see on the other side of the Neva.

The sky was grey and the snow, hundreds upon hundreds of acres of it, seemed to lie ominously silent and white.

It made, Alida thought, mankind seem puny and insignificant, and she imagined an eternity of such purity without any break to make it more human.

Mary and the Count had moved to another window which looked out over the roofs of the Palace to where in the distance were the spires and domes of the Liteinnoi Quarter.

The Prince stood beside Alida as if he was waiting for her to say something.

"It is so white, so impersonal . . . so cold," she said, "that it is frightening!"

"And yet there can be fire on the snow," he replied.

His answer surprised her and she looked up at him wondering what he could mean.

She thought at first he would have explained his words, but almost abruptly, as if he forced himself to do so, he turned aside to draw Mary's attention to the preparations there were being made in front of the Palace for the Ball that evening.

"Fire on the snow," Alida repeated almost beneath her breath.

Then petulantly Mary insisted that she and Count Ivan must start on their sight-seeing tour of the City.

The Ball was more beautiful and more glamourously exciting than even Alida had expected.

It was the first big Ball she had ever been to, and although she had accompanied Mary to several parties given by their neighbours in Hertfordshire, she had never imagined that over a thousand people could dance in one great room.

She had been excited from the moment that she realised that the Prince intended her to be present and had, with what she thought was a most astute cleverness, provided her with a gown.

She could hardly believe it was true when at six o'clock in the evening a dress-maker had come to her bed-room carrying a gown which except for a few superficial amendments fitted her perfectly.

It was so lovely that Alida felt for a moment that there must have been some mistake and it could not be intended for her.

The woman who had made the gown was French and had, she told Alida, a most distinguished *clientèle* amongst the Russian Nobility.

"Only for the Grand Duchess, *Ma'm'selle*," she said, "would I have upset my whole work-room to make two gowns at such a speed and without any warning."

"When were you told they were required, *Madame?*" Alida asked.

"At half after one, *Ma'm'selle!*" the French woman cried. "Can you imagine? Five and a half hours in which to complete two such elegant and fantastic creations, and yet how could I refuse such a gracious lady?"

"Her Royal Highness is so kind," Alida murmured.

"I will let you into a secret, Ma'm'selle," the French woman said confidentially. "The other gown was already almost completed. It was intended for the Countess Roshoshka, but she does not require it for another week and by that time I can make her another almost identical."

She threw up her hands.

"*Mais voilà!* Your dress had to be different! See the tulle, *Ma'm'selle*, which comes from France, the silk which is from China, and the ribbons which are of a quality you are unlikely to find again."

"It is very lovely," Alida answered almost reverently.

After the severity of her grey dresses, the gown she now wore made her feel as if she were dressed in a celestial cloud.

It had a new crinoline of French whale-bone, so light and yet so perfectly balanced that it gave the dress an artistry which she knew could never have been achieved by an English dress-maker.

Her waist looked tiny and her bertha of lace, sparkling and glimmering with *diamanté,* seemed so unsubstantial that it might have been made by fairy's fingers.

And this was only to be the background for the orchids which were to be affixed at the last moment!

Bunches of them Alida learned, were to catch up the soft folds of tulle. They were also to ornament the ends of the ribbons which encircled her small waist and fell down over the wide skirt to give it a *chic* which she had never seen before.

"It is so beautiful," Alida said almost to herself, "I cannot believe it is mine."

"You will look beautiful in it, *Ma'm'selle,*" the French woman said, pleased by her enthusiasm. "If you are not the Belle of the Ball I shall be very disappointed."

When the white roses had been attached to Mary's gown she looked very English and very beautiful.

Her pink and white skin, her blue eyes, and her golden hair, which was encircled by a wreath of white roses, made her look sensational even amongst the beauties of the Russian Court.

Yet there was something cold and statuesque about her which, although Alida did not realise it, made people turn almost with a sense of relief to look at the girl whom they had previously dismissed in their minds as "the unimportant English cousin."

Excitement had brought a sparkle to Alida's eyes and a smile to her lips which seemed to make her come alive.

She glowed, and once a man had looked at her sensitive little face it was hard for him to turn his eyes away.

She felt that it was almost sacrilege to use the Prince's precious star orchids. The maids pinned them onto her dress and attached them to the glittering bertha.

They then arranged just two perfect blooms on the curls as the back of her head.

She looked very young and very innocent, and at the same time there was something infectious about her enjoyment that was irresistible.

Alida had hoped that she would be asked to dance, but she had not expected to be besieged by partners.

Yet they were fighting for her favours from the moment the Ball had begun with the polonaises and mazurkas, to the time when the waltzes started.

She even found almost to her consternation that she was having to refuse those who beseeched her for "just one dance."

She was not quite certain how it happened, but she had a suspicion that he had manoeuvred it when she found herself dancing with the General.

To her surprise he danced well, yet it gave her a feeling of repugnance when his arm encircled her waist and his hand touched hers.

She could not forget the manner in which he had spoken of the punishment he would inflict on the Cadet who had made a mistake at the Parade.

Despite the excitement over her gown, a feeling of horror had remained at the back of her mind since the morning when Mary had watched a man being flogged.

"You are enjoying yourself, Miss Shenley?"

It seemed to Alida that the General's words were a statment of fact rather than a question.

"I have never enjoyed anything so much as this wonderful Ball," she answered.

"You will enjoy mine more," he said. "It is taking place tomorrow night, as of course you know."

"Yes, I had heard that you were giving one at your Palace," Alida replied. "Thank you for inviting me."

"It will please you!" he said positively.

To her relief the dance then came to an end and she was claimed by another partner.

It was only as the evening was almost at an end that she realised why she had a little ache in her heart which should not have been there. It was because the Prince had not asked her to dance.

She had thought at first that he was determined not to make her conspicuous by his attentions, as Count Ivan was doing with Mary.

Then as the hours passed and partner succeeded partner, she told herself that it must be because he did not really want to dance with her.

Somehow she had thought that he would understand, after what they had said to each other last night, that for her to dance with him would be a wonderful experience.

She could not help watching him move round the room, realising he had a grace that was indescribable!

Tall men were often clumsy, but the Prince would, she thought, be incapable of making any movement that was not rhythmic and elegant.

Yet while he was handsome to the point where his contemporaries teased him, no-one could possibly suggest that he was anything but completely and outstandingly masculine.

He wore a military uniform which was immensely becoming. The thigh-length white tunic was frogged with gold and trimmed at the neck, wrists, and hem with blue Siberian fox. His breast glittered with orders.

Alida watched him dance with the Grand Duchess, with Mary, and with various other women, yet he never approached her.

'Why? Why has he not asked me?' she wondered.

She knew that because he ignored her the whole evening was spoilt for her, even though it was the most marvellous Ball she could have imagined.

It was nearly three o'clock in the morning before the last guests said good-bye, and the last of the great conclave of sleighs outside the front door moved away.

The Grand Duchess gave a sigh of sheer weariness.

"You girls must be exhausted!" she said. "I do not think either of you stopped dancing for one second."

She looked at Mary as she spoke, and Alida wondered if Her Royal Highness was contemplating a rebuke because Mary had danced so many times with Count Ivan.

It had not escaped the notice of the other guests. In fact Alida had heard several spiteful comments about it.

The Grand Duchess led the way up the marble stairway from the Ball-Room which was on the ground floor.

"I will find my way to my own room," she smiled. "You go to yours, undress quickly, and get into bed. I do not want you heavy-eyed when you will be attending another Ball tomorrow night, and one practically every night next week. At this Season of the year all the Palaces vie with each other in the way of entertainment."

"Which is lovely for us, Ma'am!" Mary said.

"You were very much admired, my dear," the Grand Duchess told her.

Mary curtseyed and set off without a backwards glance at Alida.

"And you, Alida," the Grand Duchess said softly, "looked like some fairy creation from another land. There was no woman in the whole Ball-Room who could hold a candle to you."

Alida's eyes were wide.

"Did you . . . really think so, Ma'am?" she asked.

"It is the truth," the Grand Duchess assured her. "And I know without your telling me how much you have enjoyed yourself tonight."

"I can never thank you enough for my wonderful gown," Alida said.

"Do not thank *me*," the Grand Duchess replied meaningfully. "Good night, my child, and sleep well."

She started to turn away, then gave a little exclamation.

"What is it, Ma'am?" Alida asked.

"I have left the satin bag which matches my gown downstairs," the Grand Duchess replied. "It is not in

the Ball-Room. I remember I used it when I was sitting out in the Armoury on a sofa by the window. I
must have left it there. It contains a letter that I
would not wish any of the servants to read."

"I will fetch it for you," Alida said quickly.

She was well aware that the Grand Duchess was
implying that if one of the servants found the bag
and the letter it would undoubtedly be shown to the
Third Section of the Secret Chancellory.

"Yes, do that for me," the Grand Duchess said quietly, "but it might cause comment if you brought it to
my room tonight. Keep it safe until tomorrow."

"I will, Ma'am," Alida replied.

She curtseyed. Then, because she knew that the
Grand Duchess was worried, she hurried as quickly
as she could down the staircase and along the many
corridors which led towards the Ball-Room.

The servants had already snuffed out a large number of the lights.

The Ball-Room had been lit with four thousand
candles, and candles had also illuminated most of the
other rooms because the Grand Duchess said they
were far more becoming to women than any other
lighting.

The Armoury would have been in darkness since
all the candles in it had been extinguished; but the
curtains over the windows which comprised one wall
of the whole room had not been drawn.

Outside, while they had been dancing, a full moon
had crept up the sky, giving the snow-covered gardens a strangely ethereal appearance.

The moonlight flowed in now through the double
diamond-paned windows, which, ornamented with
Coats of Arms and other devices, cast strange varie-
gated patterns on the uncarpeted floor.

It was quite easy for Alida to move across the great
room where the walls were hung with ancient weap-
ons set with priceless jewels, swords, daggers, and
scimitars which had been carried by warriors in the
past, and find the little bag.

It was, as the Grand Duchess had said, on the sofa
by the window. It was attached to satin ribbons

which could be looped over the wrist whilst its owner danced.

Alida arranged it now on her own arm and turned to retrace her steps through the moonlight.

The room was fragrant with the scent of lilies which were grown in great china pots and arranged in profusion against the walls.

As she reached the door Alida heard music. A piano was being played, and she could hear the murmur of voices.

She guessed that some of the gentlemen had not yet left the Ball-Room or perhaps one of the rooms adjacent to it.

The music was very beguiling: it was a waltz played by a master hand which made every note entrancing, compelling, magical.

Almost without realising it, Alida's feet carried her onto the polished floor on which the moonlight shone.

Music always made her want to dance, and now she first began to sway in time to the rhythm, until she swung round the room, her crinoline billowing round her, her arms outstretched, waltzing, waltzing, waltzing in an enchanted world!

A world where there were no shadows, no cruelty, no fear.

Then as her dancing feet seemed hardly to touch the ground, and her eyes half-shut with the ecstasy of the moment, she no longer danced alone.

She felt her heart give a wild throb of excitement and she knew that this was what she had longed for all the evening.

This was what she had known it would be like to be in his arms, to know that they could move together as one person, perfectly matched and, for a moment at least, a part of each other.

Round and round the Prince swung Alida, round and round until the music stopped.

They too came to a stand-still and he stood with his back to the window so that his face was in shadow, but the moonlight was full on Alida.

Her eyes looking up at him were deep, dark pools of mystery, her lips were parted, and it was not only the exertion of the dance which made the soft lace of her gown move a little tempestuously over her breasts.

For a moment it was impossible to speak until in a voice that hardly seemed to be her own Alida whispered very softly:

"Thank . . . you."

She thought he would understand that she was thanking him not only for the dance, her gown, and the orchids, but also for so many things she could not express.

The Prince did not answer, but slowly, as if it was inescapable, as if nothing could prevent it, he drew her closer to him.

Then as her eyes looked up into his he bent his head and his lips found hers.

It was a movement that was as rhythmic as the music to which they had danced. It was a wonder as unearthly and exquisite as the silver moonlight coming through the windows.

Alida felt her lips quiver beneath his.

As if this moment had been inevitable since the beginning of time, she felt her mouth become a part of him and her whole being surrender itself.

Alida had never been kissed before, yet the rapture and wonder that flowed through her whole body was something half-remembered, something that had been there since the moment of creation.

He held her close, so close that she could hardly breathe, until as she felt that his lips made her a part of the moonlight, the lilies, the music, and himself, she was suddenly free.

He faded into the shadows as swiftly as he had come, and almost before she realised what had happened.

It was like waking from a dream, and yet she knew that her whole body pulsated with the wonder of it.

It had not been a dream, but reality!

Chapter Seven

Alida found it impossible to sleep.

She lay in bed feeling herself thrill and thrill again as she thought of her waltz with the Prince and the strange, wild feelings he had evoked when his lips touched hers.

She had not realised that a kiss could be something so alive, or that every nerve in one's body would pulsate with the wonder and glory of it.

She had known when he touched her—and she thought now that she must have known it since the first moment they met—that she was truly a part of him.

This was love! This was what she had always dreamt she would feel one day for a man, and now it had happened!

Then as the splendour of it encompassed her like a shining light, she remembered that the Prince belonged to Mary!

It felt like diving from the very heights of Heaven down into the darkness of a Hell so dark that it was without hope!

"I love him, I love him!" she whispered to herself.

And she knew with a certainty that could not be defined that she would never love anyone else. She was like her mother, who could love only once in her life-time.

"There were many men who admired me, Alida," she had said to her daughter once. "Many men who sent me flowers and paid me court, but I was very strictly brought up, and I never went out alone with any of them."

119

She smiled.

"People suspected me of living a gay life, but actually it was very dull. When I had finished dancing at the Theatre, I went home."

"And then you met Papa," Alida prompted.

"I met your father when there was a Command Performance for the Emperor of Austria. After the performance was over, he came backstage and all the cast was presented to him. He had a big entourage and many Diplomats with him, your Papa was amongst them."

"And the moment you met Papa, you fell in love?" Alida asked breathlessly.

"I think we knew, as soon as we looked into each other's eyes, there could never be anyone else for either of us," her mother had answered softly.

"And that is what I feel about the Prince," Alida told herself now. "But Papa was unmarried . . . he was free!"

It was a commitment just as binding as if Mary already wore his ring upon her finger.

"I must forget him," Alida told herself.

But she knew it was impossible. At the same time, even if she never saw the Prince again, she would never be ashamed of her love for him.

This was not infatuation, a mere passing excitement of the senses. This was a love so strong, so deep, that she felt it had existed through time itself.

Then like a dagger in her heart she asked herself if he felt the same way about her. Perhaps, after all, to him she was just another pretty girl. Someone with whom—because he was making a marriage of convenience—he could flirt besides having a wife.

"It is not true!" she whispered aloud.

She was as sure as if he told her so that there was nothing sordid about their feeling for each other.

Instead there was an indescribable magic, a bond which drew them together and which was so beautiful, so much part of the Divine that it was indefinable.

'As soon as Mary is married,' Alida thought, 'I shall be sent home and then I shall never see him again.'

It was a physical agony to know that this was what would happen and nothing could prevent it.

She must go back to the greyness, the unhappiness, and the miseries of the Castle, and Mary would bear the Prince's name and, perhaps, his children.

It was at that moment Alida felt the tears come into her eyes and run down her cheeks.

As the hours of the night passed slowly, she stared into the darkness, and reliving again that moment when the Prince had held her in his arms and they had waltzed round the Armoury.

Then he had kissed her!

She had thought that the new day would bring a fresh sense of hopelessness. However, as soon as it was light, she rose from her bed and dressed.

She knew, although she would not admit it to herself, that because she was hoping to see the Prince sometime during the day her feet would not keep still, but must carry her towards him!

She went to the wardrobe to find her grey dress with the white collar and cuffs. As she opened the door she saw hanging there the gown she had worn last night—the beautiful white tulle with its glittering bertha and fresh flowers.

Surprisingly, the orchids were not brown and wrinkled now, as she had expected, but seemed to have retained their freshness.

She looked at their little star-shaped faces and thought that the mere fact that they were still so alive and lovely brought her a message of hope!

Then she told herself that she was being nonsensical.

"I have to face facts," she murmured. "The Prince will be Mary's husband, and although I love him with all my heart and soul, I can never tell him so."

She was sure that it was a deliberate decision on his part the night before not to speak to her.

He must have come unexpectedly into the Armoury, and finding her dancing by herself had on an impulse joined her. Perhaps his kiss had been on impulse too?

And yet Alida felt certain that something greater than themselves had drawn them together.

She had only to shut her eyes to see his head and broad shoulders silhouetted against the moonlight coming in through the windows, to feel again as if her voice was lost in her throat, to know that what was happening was so exciting that it was impossible to breathe!

"I love him," she said aloud.

Bending forward, she kissed very gently the petals of one of the white orchids he had picked for her.

Then resolutely she forced herself to shut away her dream-world which could never become reality.

She closed the wardrobe door and put on her severe grey-cotton gown with its puritanical collar and cuffs.

It was still very early. Mary, she knew, would still be asleep. Alida moved quietly into the Sitting-Room, thinking she would find a book and try to read until the rest of the house was stirring.

She had not forgotten the little satin bag which belonged to the Grand Duchess.

She had hidden it very carefully in the bottom of one of her drawers beneath her under-clothes, where she felt it was most unlikely that one of the maids would find it.

Martha attended to Mary, but Alida was waited on by two apple-cheeked Russian peasant girls who came from the country, and it was impossible to imagine that they were intelligent enough to spy on anyone.

In any case, she only half-credited everything she had been told about the all-persuasive power of the Third Section of the Secret Chancellory, or the surveillance of the Secret Police.

It seemed impossible in the comfort of the Palace to believe in them.

Whatever she might have felt when she was listening to Mr. Tatkenski, she was almost certain now that a great many of the tales were a "bogey" with which the Russians deliberately scared themselves.

She found in the Sitting-Room a book which interested her, and sitting down in the comfortable seat by the tiled stove, she turned over the pages.

But after a few moments she realised that she had not read a word. Her memories of last night kept intruding upon her.

The door of the Sitting-Room opened and she thought it must be a servant coming to tidy the room, or perhaps, as happened at frequent intervals, to add more birch-wood to the stove.

Then, turning her head, she saw that a footman was standing in the doorway, gesticulating.

Alida had already found that whilst few Russian servants could speak any language but their own, they were extremely astute at understanding mime.

She had learnt to express with her hands what she desired, and almost immediately, it seemed, they did what was required of them.

Now the flunkey in his red uniform was beckoning with his gloved hand. Alida rose to her feet and walked towards him.

"Cum," he said in a low voice. "Cum."

Surprised, Alida followed him, and he set off at a quick pace down the corridor.

She thought that perhaps the Grand Duchess was sending for her and wondered if she should have brought the satin bag with her. But it was still very early—too early, she thought, for the Grand Duchess to be awake.

The flunkey led her to the top of the Grand Staircase and then, instead of crossing in the direction of the Grand Duchess's apartments, descended the stairs.

Alida followed him wonderingly, until on reaching the Hall she saw to her surprise that Count Ivan was standing there.

He was resplendent in his uniform and, from the way he looked up at her as she came down the Staircase, he had obviously been waiting impatiently for her arrival.

It went through Alida's mind that he had something of importance to convey to Mary and that she was to be his messenger! But when she reached his side he said surprisingly:

"I want you to come with me."

. . "Where to?" Alida enquired.

"I will tell you later," he replied. "It is unnecessary for me to say that it is important, otherwise I should not have called so early in the morning."

"Do explain . . ." Alida began, only to realise that with a snap of his fingers Count Ivan had commanded the servants to hurry forward with fur-lined boots, a fur cape, and a fur hood turned back with a facing of white sable.

"These are not mine," Alida protested.

"There are always furs in the Hall for those who need them." Count Ivan replied.

As he spoke he donned a huge fur coat over his uniform and set a fur cap at a jaunty angle on one side of his dark-haired head.

"Where are we going?" Alida enquired again, breathless from the speed at which she had been dressed.

But already the Count had preceded her through the front door of the Palace and down the steps to where a sleigh was waiting. Drawn by four black horses and painted with the Benkendorf Coat of Arms, it was exceedingly impressive.

Alida had realised by now that everyone of importance in St. Petersburg had a four-horse carriage, a barouche, brougham, travelling-carriages, droshkies, and four-horse and single sleighs.

The rugs in Count Ivan's sleigh were of sable, and it seemed to Alida that it was more richly cushioned and more luxurious even than those belonging to the Grand Duchess.

There were two Coachmen on the box, and as soon as the flunkeys had finished arranging the rugs, they set off at a great pace.

"Where are you taking me?" Alida asked again, and now there was a little note of fear in her voice.

She did not know why, but she thought that Count Ivan looked grim, and his face in the early morning light seemed older and harsher than it did at other times.

"Everything will be explained when we reach our destination," he said in a suppressive tone.

Alida subsided into silence because she had the feeling that however many questions she asked, they would not be answered.

It was also very cold which made speech more difficult. There had been a further fall of snow during the night and now the City was wholly white, whilst only the domes and spires glittered with a kind of crystalline brilliance which came from the particles of frost on the snow.

They had not a very long way to go, only down a broad thoroughfare which Alida had already traversed several times.

Then the sleigh came to a stand-still in front of a large building with a great flight of steps leading up to it and huge columns over the entrance.

There were soldiers on guard and Alida decided that it must be a Palace of some sort.

Servants ran to assist her alight, and she walked up the steps beside the Count and in through a huge door which led to a marble Hall.

There was the usual abundance of flunkeys to take their fur coats from them and unfasten Alida's fur boots.

By the time she was free of her wraps, she found that the Count had already walked some way ahead of her, and when she joined him they proceeded in silence down the broad corridor which was uncarpeted.

The sound of their feet seemed to echo eerily and Alida in her grey dress and with uncovered head felt small and defenceless.

She had always been sensitive to smell.

Although it was very warm indoors, there was something that smelled sour and dank about this place to which she could not put a name.

Suddenly she knew that it was—it was the smell of fear!

They had walked a long way and she said to Count Ivan:

"I must insist that you tell me where we are going. I think perhaps I should not have come with you without asking the permission of the Grand Duchess."

"There was no reason for you to ask her permission," the Count replied sharply.

"I am her guest," Alida insisted.

The Count did not respond and she asked:

"What is this building?"

"It is His Majesty's Chancellory."

Alida stood still. The Count walked on a few paces and then, realising that she had stopped, turned back.

"Come along!" he ordered almost roughly.

"What Chancellory?" Alida asked.

He looked at her with an expression in his face that she did not understand and then he said:

"It is not of importance, but there is someone here waiting to see you."

"Someone from the Third Section?" Alida asked.

"What do you know about that?" the Count enquired.

"Why have you ... brought me ... here?" Alida demanded, and now there was a little tremor in her voice.

"Everything will be explained to you. General Dubbett is waiting," Count Ivan replied.

Alida drew in her breath. She knew now, incredible though it might be, that she had been brought here for questioning.

She had not believed it possible that it could happen to her, a British subject, and yet the fact that she had been hurried away from the Michailow Palace by the Count in this surreptitious manner could mean only one thing.

It was then, as she walked slowly to join Count Ivan, that she told herself she must not be afraid, and just as if someone had told her what was about to happen, she knew that she was about to be interrogated about Mr. Tatkenski.

The Secret Police would have seen her on the Quay, she thought, and even as she thought it she knew that, whatever happened, she must not involve the Prince.

Count Ivan already hated him. Mary had told her that.

Alida was quite certain that the Count would be

only too glad to make trouble for the man who was championing the emancipation of the Serfs.

Alida drew in her breath and told herself that she must remain calm.

But insidiously there crept into her mind the stories her father had told of how people were questioned about their activities.

Of cruelties that were inflicted by the representatives of one country on those of another, and how Secret Agents would be tortured until they implicated their associates.

'I must be very polite,' Alida admonished herself. 'I must answer the questions and tell the truth . . . wherever it is possible.'

Somewhere from the past she heard the echo of her father's voice saying:

"One of the great arts of disguise, and incidentally one of the arts of diplomacy, is to tell the truth whenever one can, and if one has to tell a lie, then to tell a good one!"

He had laughed as he spoke and Alida knew he was joking, and yet now his words seemed to come to her almost like a personal message.

'Whoever else is implicated,' she thought, 'it must not be the Prince.'

She knew now that she had always disliked Count Ivan. In fact she had hated him from the moment that he behaved so outrageously with Mary on the *Maid of Hull.*

It had been so easy for a man as experienced and, in his own way, as attractive as he was to seduce a girl like Mary, who was desperately anxious to escape from the restrictions of her father and mother, and who had a craving to be flattered and admired.

How could she resist the Count, who knew every move of the game, and who had singled her out in a most compromising manner from the moment they had met.

'Perhaps,' Alida thought, 'it is part of his desire for revenge on the Prince that has made Count Ivan behave like this. It would be a subtle revenge to entice the future bride of Prince Vorontski into his arms before the Prince has even set eyes on her!'

It was not only because he was a libertine that Alida hated Count Ivan. She knew that he was cruel and relentless and that he would stop at nothing to get his own way.

Somehow, by some means, he would prevent the Tsar from giving the Serfs their freedom, and the Grand Duchess had made it very plain that his chief opponent, the man who had the ear of the Emperor Alexander, was the Prince.

As they reached the end of the long passage and turned into another one Alida's heart was beating so loudly that she felt the Count must hear it.

Here, outside enormous double doors, stood two sentries who sprang to attention at the sight of them. The doors opened as they approached and they entered a big, bare Ante-Room in which there were a number of persons seated on long benches.

The Count did not pause, but Alida could not help looking at them as they sat there obviously waiting for attention.

She realised that, strangely, they evinced no curiosity about her. They majority of them did not even raise their heads as she and the Count passed them.

They just sat there on the benches, men and women, staring sightlessly into space, or looking despondently at the floor.

'They are people without hope,' Alida thought. 'They know what is awaiting them and that there is no escape.'

She felt another little tremor of fear run through her; then she told herself that she was British. It would be impossible for her to disappear as Mr. Tatkenski might do. And even if there was an unfortunate accident, the Grand Duchess would undoubtedly make enquiries. And so would the Prince.

At the thought of him a wave of courage seemed to sweep over Alida.

'He would be brave in such circumstances,' she thought, 'and I must be the same.'

They crossed the long room with its miserable occupants and now two other doors guarded by sentries were opened. These led into an impressive-looking office with high windows on one side, the other walls being decorated with maps.

At the far end of the room, seated at a huge black desk, was a man wearing the pale-blue uniform of the Secret Police.

It was a long way to walk to the desk, and Alida told herself that this was all part of the intimidation of anyone who was brought here for interrogation.

The whole room was designed to make a person feel insignificant, and yet General Dubbett, when he rose to greet the Count, was not a particularly impressive man.

Alida forced herself to look at him dispassionately, and she knew immediately that he was not an Aristocrat or even what an Englishman would call a "gentlemen."

His face had high cheek-bones and deep lines, and without being clairvoyant she could see in his expression secretiveness, cruelty, and a love of intrigue.

She found too, as his eyes turned towards her, that there was mockery in the penetrating glance he gave her.

"Miss Shenley," he said and bowed. "I am grateful to you for coming here this morning."

"I had little choice, General," Alida replied with what she hoped was a composure she was far from feeling.

"Will you be seated?"

The General shuffled some papers in his hands and, faced the light. She sat down on the edge of it, making every effort to appear at ease.

She knew that it would be a mistake to be over-tense, and she forced herself to think of the way the Prince had waltzed with her the night before, and almost immediately she felt more relaxed.

The General shuffled some papers in his hands and, without looking at her, said:

"I wanted you to come here, Miss Shenley, as you are the only person who can help us on a very serious matter."

"What can that be?" Alida asked, hoping that there was the right amount of surprise in her voice.

"It concerns a man who is an enemy of the State, a man with whom you had a conversation on board the *Maid of Hull*. His name is Tatkenski."

"Yes, of course, I remember him," Alida replied.

The General suddenly raised his face from his papers and said sharply, so sharply that Alida almost jumped:

"Why did you go to the Quay yesterday morning to meet the *Bosporos*?"

"A piece of my baggage was left behind at Kiel," Alida said quietly. "I imagined the authorities would be kind enough to forward it on the next ship coming to St. Petersburg."

"How could this important piece of baggage have gone astray between the *Maid of Hull* and the Royal Yacht?" General Dubbett asked.

Alida smiled.

"I have no idea," she answered. "It was quite a small piece and I expect it was left behind in my cabin."

"Surely your maid could have gone to the Quay to identify it?" the General suggested.

Alida shook her head.

"The maid we brought from England attends only on my cousin, Lady Mary. She was not my maid in England and did not pack for me before we left. If the label was missing, as I rather suspected, I doubt whether she would have been able to identify the bag."

The General was silent for a moment and Alida realised that the Count, sitting beside him, opposite her, was watching her closely.

She forced herself to give him a little smile and said:

"I always think it is amazing that more baggage is not lost on long journeys. When one has a lot of changes, it is very easy for something to be overlooked."

The Count made no comment and the General, as if he felt that Alida was ignoring him, interposed:

"When you spoke to this man Tatkenski on the *Maid of Hull*, did he tell you when he was arriving in St. Petersburg?"

It was, Alida knew, a trick question, and she managed to answer without a moment's hesitation:

"But Mr. Tatkenski told me he was going to Stockholm."

"Did he tell you why?"

Alida shook her head.

"Did he tell you he was trying to find his mother?"

"He told me his father was dead," Alida replied. "I understand he was sent to Siberia."

"He was a revolutionary, an anarchist," the General said harshly.

"Mr. Tatkenski is now a British Citizen," Alida remarked.

"So he told you that! Yes, that is true, for what it is worth," the General remarked dryly. "I suppose you are aware we have in Russia ways of making people tell us what we want to know?"

"What method do you use?" Alida asked with a laughing note in her voice. "Thumb screws which England discarded in Elizabethan times? Or the rack which the Spaniards used in the Inquisition?"

She smiled and added in a slightly mocking tone:

"I am sure my Uncle, the Duke of Berkhampstead, who is often in attendance on the Queen, and my Aunt, who is related to many of the Royal families of Europe, will be very surprised if I return to England six inches taller and without my thumbs!"

She saw that the Count was astonished by the manner in which she spoke. The General merely drummed his fingers on the desk before he said sharply:

"Now, Miss Shenley, tell me what Mr. Tatkenski looked like when he disembarked from the *Bosporos*."

Alida stared at him.

"Was Mr. Tatkenski on the *Bosporos*?" she asked.

"I am asking the questions," the General replied.

"But I have just told you that he was going to Sweden," Alida answered.

"You say you did not see him disembark, and yet

you stood at the foot of the gang-plank watching the passengers come ashore."

"I was not watching them but simply waiting for them to disembark before I went on board," Alida said. "There is not enough room on a gang-plank for two people to walk in different directions at the same time."

"I am aware of that!" the General snapped. "Are you telling me you did not notice Tatkenski?"

"I cannot keep repeating the same thing over and over again," Alida said with a little touch of irritation in her voice. "Mr. Tatkenski told me he was going to Sweden, and I saw no reason why I should disbelieve it. So why should I pay any attention to the passengers disembarking yesterday?"

Her voice softened.

"I was sorry for him because he told me his father was dead—brutally murdered in Siberia. I am afraid, General, that I am unable to help you further, and I think I should now return to the Palace before my cousin begins to wonder what has happened to me."

She rose to her feet as she spoke and saw a faint flicker of surprise on the General's face.

He glanced at Count Ivan and the Count said in a tone which Alida felt was imperative:

"Did Prince Vorontski tell you how deeply he sympathised with Mr. Tatkenski?"

"Does he sympathise with him?" Alida enquired. "But how?"

"Did the Prince tell you that Mr. Tatkenski was coming to Russia to find his mother?" the General enquired.

"Is Mr. Tatkenski's mother still alive?" Alida exclaimed. "He said he had not been in Russia for fifteen years, and surely after that long time, if he had not heard from her, he would expect her to be dead."

She sighed.

"I was so sorry for him. He seemed so sad and he had been so ill. I was trying to express my sympathy for him when Count Ivan saw us together in the Saloon."

"Yes, yes, I have been told all that," General Dubbett said. "What I am trying to discover, Miss Shenley, is where Mr. Tatkenski is likely to be at this moment."

"I am afraid there is nothing I can tell you that would be of the slightest help," Alida said, "unless of course you send someone to Stockholm. It should not be difficult to find him if he was on board any ship which sailed from Kiel bound for the Swedish Capital."

The General made an exasperated sound and looked at Count Ivan.

"This enquiry, Count," he said, "it is getting us nowhere."

"I am quite convinced," Count Ivan replied, "that Prince Vorontski will help Tatkenski if he arrived in Russia. He has helped such men before."

"We have never been able to prove it," General Dubbett remarked.

"I shall prove it sooner or later!" Count Ivan retorted. "I think it extremely strange for Miss Shenley to take the trouble to rise so early in the morning to go to meet the *Bosporos* when any servant in the Palace could quite easily have collected her baggage for her."

Alida gave a sigh of impatience.

"I thought I had already explained," she said, "there was no-one who could have identified the bag except myself. Besides, Count, as you well know, Martha was very ill on the *Maid of Hull* and she has not been feeling well since we arrived.

"It was really no trouble for me to go to the Quay, and I positively enjoyed the drive through the City. It was the first time I had ever been in a sleigh."

She turned her face towards General Dubbett and forced a smile to her lips.

"I think riding in a sleigh is the most romantic mode of travel I have ever known. I am so lucky to be in St. Petersburg when there is snow on the ground."

General Dubbett rose to his feet.

"I think, Miss Shenley, I need not detain you any longer. May I thank you for coming here? If you do hear anything from Mr. Tatkenski, or about him, perhaps you would be kind enough to let me know."

"I cannot imagine why he should get in touch with me," Alida replied lightly.

She moved towards the door. As she turned away she heard Count Ivan say to the General in a low voice:

"Are you quite certain she is telling the truth?"

Without turning round to see, she had the feeling that the General gave a shrug of his shoulders. Then Count Ivan came striding after her across the floor and they reached the double doors together.

They walked back along the passages in silence to where the servants were waiting to help them into their furs.

Only when they had moved away from the Chancellory did Count Ivan say with what Alida thought was a note of apology in his voice:

"I hope you understand that men like Tatkenski are enemies of the State. They cannot be permitted to go undetected."

"Of course I understand," Alida said sweetly. "I am sure His Majesty must appreciate your vigilance in this matter. I expect the Grand Duchess will be equally grateful when I tell her about it."

There was a moment's pause, and then Count Ivan said:

"I would like to ask a favour of you."

"Yes?" Alida enquired.

"I would rather you did not mention to the Grand Duchess where we have been this morning. She is, as you know, friends with Nicholas Miliutin, who makes a great deal of trouble over such incidents."

Alida said nothing and Count Ivan went on:

"Miliutin has Communist leanings. He was at the dinner the night you arrived, and my father was exceedingly surprised to see him there."

"I am afraid I cannot remember what he looked like," Alida said.

"Then keep away from him," Count Ivan warned, "and promise me you will say nothing of having met

General Dubbett either to Her Royal Highness or to Prince Vorontski."

"I think you take rather a lot upon yourself, Count Ivan," Alida replied. "Is it not unusual for English visitors to be interrogated in such a manner without protection and without even a Chaperon?"

"That is true," Count Ivan said, "which is why I am asking you for your cousin's sake not to repeat what has happened this morning."

Alida raised her eye-brows.

"For my cousin's sake?"

"There is no reason why Mary should be involved in this," the Count murmured.

"Of course not," Alida agreed. "She never spoke to Mr. Tatkenski, whilst I am under suspicion because I spoke a few words of sympathy to a stranger who was obviously suffering!"

The Count made no reply and Alida added:

"What a strange country this is where suspicion can be aroused by such a simple action!"

With intent she had spoken scathingly, and then to her relief she saw that they had already reached the Michailow Palace.

"I hope I can rely on your discretion," the Count said.

Alida drew in her breath.

"I only wish I could rely on yours, Count Ivan."

She looked him in the eyes as she spoke, and before he could reply to what she knew was an impertinence on her part, she alighted from the sleigh and hurried up the steps of the Palace.

It was still very early and when she reached the Sitting-Room she gathered that Mary had not yet been called.

It was then for the first time she felt cold and frightened.

It was terrifying to think of where she had been, and that Count Ivan, because of his hatred of the Prince, should have subjected her to such an ordeal.

That was the key to everything she knew! The Count's hatred of the Prince! She must warn him.

Then she prayed that Mr. Tatkenski would find his

mother, and somehow the Prince would enable them to disappear from Russia. But if they were caught, the Prince would be involved, and then what would be the consequences?

Alida found herself shivering and went near to the stove.

Somehow she must warn the Prince. She knew that never again, except in his private apartments, would she feel safe from listening ears, from spies who must lurk everywhere, even inside the Palace itself.

A Senior-servant was sent to tell them that they were to have luncheon early.

"I know why," Mary said with glee when she finally appeared about noon. "The Grand Duchess is taking us to the Winter Palace this afternoon to see the Empress's jewels."

"How exciting!" Alida exclaimed.

But she did not feel excited. She felt only concern for the Prince.

At luncheon, which was in the small Dining-Room, he was not present. Alida on entering the room handed the Grand Duchess the satin bag she had fetched from the Armoury last night.

"I made a silly mistake, Ma'am," she said in a clear voice so that the servants could hear. "I picked up your bag last night as well as my own. The Ball was so thrilling, I am afraid I was not thinking clearly."

"I wondered what I could have done with it!" the Grand Duchess exclaimed. "Thank you, my dear, for keeping it safely."

She put it in another bag which she carried over her arm and then sat down to luncheon.

On the way to the Winter Palace in the big sleigh which held all three of them in comfort, Alida wondered how she could tell the Grand Duchess that she wanted to see the Prince alone.

She was too frightened to speak when there was anyone else within hearing, and it seemed during the afternoon almost impossible for them not to be surrounded by people.

The Winter Palace was as remarkable and impressive as Alida had expected. Joined to the Hermitage and built by the Empress Elizabeth in 1762, it was one immense, solid mass of building.

"It houses six thousand people," the Duchess told them.

"So many!" Alida exclaimed in awe-struck tones.

"Her Majesty has two hundred *Dames d'honneur* always in waiting, and there are four hundred cooks!" the Grand Duchess told her.

"The food should be good!" Alida laughed.

There were so many magnificent and precious things to see as they moved towards the Empress's private apartments that Alida felt it would take a life-time for anyone to take in even a quarter of them.

Just as in the Michailow Palace, the bright, Italian-painted ceilings were breath-taking and there was a collection of vases, tables, and pedestals of jasper, porphyry, jade, and malachite, each one more perfect and more valuable than the last.

There were pictures, some of the most treasured in the whole world, and the silver tables, lights, and sconces in the Throne-Room were dazzling.

"What I would like you to see, if there is time," the Grand Duchess said as they moved along the corridor, "is the Orangerie, which is very lovely. What is unusual is that it is a complete garden on the first floor."

The Grand Duchess smiled.

"As you will have realised by now, we have very long Winters and much of the time we are unable to go outside. So in most Russian houses you will find masses of cultivated flowers."

"I was very impressed," Alida said, "by the flowers in your Conservatory, Ma'am."

"The gardens here are even more surprising," the Grand Duchess answered. "Trees which are grown in square boxes and heated in a special way are sometimes over thirty feet high, and there is a lawn which by frequent watering is kept fresh all the year long, interspersed with flower-beds."

She smiled.

"I think really the Prince ought to show you the garden in the Palace because it was his idea to have a most ingenious arrangement of lamps so that the impression of either sunlight or moonlight can be produced."

"How extraordinary!" Alida exclaimed.

"Sometimes," the Grand Duchess continued, "in the very depths of Winter, we dance on the grass in the moonlight and sit out in Arbours covered with roses and honeysuckle."

"How fascinating!" Alida cried.

Then, before she could ask any more questions, they arrived at the Empress's private apartments.

The first Salon was small and decorated surprisingly in pink and white satin. The next which they passed through had some magnificent paintings and there was a high gilt cage with a colourful macaw inside it.

From here they entered a corner room with four windows, where the Empress was waiting for them.

She was still very beautiful, Alida thought, but she looked sad and there was a stiffness and air of isolation about her, almost as though she had withdrawn herself from the world.

Wearing a gown of Brussels lace and a little velvet cloak trimmed with ermine, she greeted the Grand Duchess with a kiss. First Mary was presented, then Alida. They sank down in deep curtseys.

"The Grand Duchess tells me you would like to see my jewellery," the Empress said in a voice that was somehow impersonal.

"I adore beautiful jewellery, Ma'am," Mary enthused.

"Then you will enjoy mine," the Empress answered.

She took them all into her bed-room, where all her magnificent jewels were displayed in large glass cases, and in a separate *armoire*, those belonging to the Crown.

The Empress explained that she was given a marvellous parure on every fête day and on the birth of every child.

"I am almost running out of stones!" she said with a faint smile as she displayed emeralds, rubies, turquoises, sapphires, pearls, and diamonds, each set larger and more magnificent than the last.

The Emperor's Crown was kept in a different part of the Palace. Surprisingly, the Empress's Crown was disappointingly small.

But there was a large diamond necklace with drops the size of pigeon's eggs and an immense ruby with a long history of adventure attached to it.

Some exquisite emeralds excited Mary, while Alida was fascinated by a quantity of beautiful, old jewelled fans.

It was difficult to take in everything at once, but Alida could not help being especially amused when she saw a tiny pistol covered completely with rubies and diamonds.

"Is that real, Ma'am?" she asked.

"It is, indeed," the Empress replied. "The Tsar gave it to me when we were first married to replace a very ordinary one I had as a girl."

"Can Your Majesty shoot?" Mary asked in a surprised voice.

"Of course I can," the Empress answered. "Most girls in Russia learn to shoot when they are young because of the wolves and bears one encounters quite often in the gardens of a country-house!"

"I am sure if I were to see a wolf I should be too frightened to pull the trigger!" Mary exclaimed.

"I see the Prince will have to teach you to handle a pistol," the Empress said. "He is noted as being an exceptional shot."

"He is indeed," the Grand Duchess agreed, "but His Highness prefers smaller game, like partridge and quail."

Alida was turning the little jewelled pistol over in her hand.

"It is so light!" she said. "I cannot believe, Ma'am, that it is possible to make anything so light which could yet be effective."

"You sound as if you have handled a pistol before," the Empress remarked.

"My father taught me when we lived in Paris," Alida explained. "He was a very good shot and he thought that if a woman travelled about the Continent she should be able to defend herself. He was not worried above wolves and bears, of course, but bandits and robbers!"

The Empress gave her a sad little smile.

"We all have our own enemies," she said, and Alida thought how true that was.

They had tea in the Empress's private Salon, which was literally covered with bijouterie and where hundreds of flowers scented the air with an exquisite fragrance.

This room had an open fire and there was a little Blenheim spaniel lying in front of it who looked very comfortable and appeared quite unimpressed at the grandeur round him.

As soon as they had finished their tea, the Empress rose to her feet.

"I am afraid I have some people waiting for me," she said to the Grand Duchess. "But we shall see you, dearest Hélène, again this evening."

"You have been gracious enough to ask me to dinner and to hear the new Opera at the Imperial Theatre," the Grand Duchess replied.

"It will be such a pleasure!" the Grand Duchess exclaimed.

"The girls are going to a Ball at the Benkendorf Palace," the Grand Duchess went on. "As I shall not be chaperoning them, Princess Radziwell has promised to take my place."

"Then they will be in good hands," the Empress said.

They made their farewells with curtseys to the ground and the Grand Duchess kissed first the Empress's hand and then her cheek.

As they drove back to the Michailow Palace in their sleigh Mary exclaimed:

"I have never seen such amazing jewels! I would give anything in the world to own diamonds or emeralds like that! Think how they would look against my skin!"

"Jewels are no substitute for an aching heart," the Grand Duchess remarked.

"You mean that Her Majesty is unhappy?" Alida asked in a low voice.

"She is always very sad," the Grand Duchess replied, "and the Emperor likes to be gay. He enjoys the company of beautiful women and, like all Russians, he continually fancies himself in love."

As she spoke she gave a little sidelong glance at Mary, and Alida knew that she was warning her that Count Ivan's interest in her was not likely to be permanent.

"Who could blame His Majesty?" Mary said in a hard voice. "But, after all, although one is sorry for the Empress if she is unhappy, she has a very great position and fantastic possessions."

"Yes, of course, she has all those," the Grand Duchess said, "but I wonder if ultimately they are any consolation."

Mary did not answer and in her heart Alida said to herself:

'The Grand Duchess is right! It is love that counts! Not position nor possessions, but love!'

She thought that she could live in a garret with someone she loved and be happy, terribly happy, if it was with the right person!

Then, as she thought of the Prince, she remembered how important it was that she should warn him about Count Ivan.

"I wonder, Ma'am," she said hesitatingly to the Grand Duchess, "if you will be seeing Mr. Stroyensky this evening?"

"I am afraid not," the Grand Duchess answered. "Mr. Stroyensky left St. Petersburg this morning for Warsaw."

"Oh, in that case," Alida exclaimed, "I wonder if you would ask the Prince whether Mr. Stroyensky left with him a piece of music which he promised me. I am sure he would not have forgotten."

The Grand Duchess gave her a searching glance.

"I will ask the Prince if he has it," she said slowly. "I am sure Mr. Stroyensky will have remembered his promise, and the Prince will arrange to bring the music to you as soon as he is free."

"Thank you, Ma'am," Alida said quietly.

But her breath came quickly between her lips and there was a sudden light in her eyes. She would see the Prince again soon!

She would see the man she loved! The man who had kissed her last night and taken her very soul into his keeping.

Chapter Eight

Alida looked at herself in the mirror with delight.

During the day the French dress-maker had come to the Palace and removed the white orchids which had decorated her tulle gown and instead had sewn on bows of shadow lace decorated with *diamanté* to match the bertha.

It made the dress glitter with every movement and also gave it a French *chic* which could never have been attained by an English gown.

Tonight there were no orchids for Alida to wear in her hair, but her eyes seemed to sparkle like diamonds and she knew as she stared at herself in the mirror that it was because, in a very short while, she would see the Prince.

She had been hoping all the evening that he would understand her message about the music left for her by Mr. Stroyensky and would contrive to meet her, but there had been no summons to the Grand Duchess's private apartments.

When it was time to start dressing for the Ball, Alida wondered despairingly if she should have taken more urgent steps to warn the Prince about Count Ivan.

'Perhaps he did not understand' she worried, and wondered how she would ever be able to see him alone.

Just before she and Mary repaired to their bedrooms, a servant wearing the green livery that proclaimed him one of the Prince's household brought them each a small bouquet to carry in their hands.

Tonight there were roses and carnations for Mary,

and for Alida, lilies-of-the-valley whose scent seemed somehow a part of her dreams.

"His Royal Higness's compliments, M'Lady," the servant said to Mary, "and he has asked me to inform Your Ladyship that he will be escorting you and Miss Shenley to the Ball."

"But Count Ivan is coming for me!" Mary exclaimed sharply.

Then as the servant left the room she said to Alida with a change of tone:

"Never mind, this means we can go in two sleighs."

As she spoke she went into her own bed-room, and Alida felt a sudden sense of excitement. To speed over the snow with the Prince would be a most wonderful experience.

There was something marvellously romantic about moving so swiftly and so silently, and there would still be a full moon, as there had been last night when they had danced together in the Armoury.

She took extra pains over arranging her fair hair and she knew that nothing could be more becoming to her air of fragility than the fairy-like tulle gown which she owed entirely to the Prince's understanding.

"I love him!" she whispered to herself. "Will he admire me?"

She knew she should not think of him in such a way, but it was impossible to have a thought which did not concern him.

"It is not wrong, for it is my secret," Alida excused herself. "And although I can be nothing of any consequence in his life, yet to me he is all the happiness I shall ever know."

When she was back at the Castle, she thought, being bullied and berated by her Uncle and Aunt, even they could not prevent her from dreaming of the Prince, from remembering his handsome face, from thanking God for his kindness to her.

"I love him," she said again. "He is all that is good and kind and noble!"

She was ready in the Sitting-Room long before Mary appeared, but when her cousin did emerge from the bed-room there was no doubt that she looked exceedingly lovely.

Tonight she was in pale blue, the colour of her eyes, and her gown, looped, ruched, and pleated over her crinoline, was trimmed with huge bunches of curled ostrich feathers in the same colour.

"You look very beautiful!" Alida exclaimed sincerely.

"What I need is some of the jewellery we saw this afternoon," Mary replied. "I can only hope the Vorontskis possess a decent tiara."

"No-one who is as beautiful as you really needs jewels."

"I need them!" Mary retorted. "I need diamonds and sapphires, emeralds and rubies! Yes, and sables too! I want all the riches that Russia can give me, and, what is more, I intend to have them!"

There was a greedy, covetous note in her voice. Alida, because it hurt her when her cousin spoke like that, said quietly:

"Do we wait here for our escorts or do we go downstairs?"

"I imagine the servants will tell us when Count Ivan arrives," Mary replied.

At that moment the door opened.

"He must be here!" she exclaimed.

One of the Grand Duchess's Senior-servants, a Major-Domo who wore an even more resplendent livery than that of the other staff, came into the room.

He was an elderly man and spoke extremely good English.

"I have to inform you, M'Lady," he said to Mary, "that it will not be possible for you to attend the Ball tonight."

"Not attend the Ball?" Mary repeated with a little cry. "What do you mean?"

"His Highness Prince Vorontski has asked me to inform you, M'Lady, that the route is dangerous and he hopes therefore in Her Royal Highness's absence that you will allow him to entertain you and Miss Shenley at dinner."

"I do not believe that it is impossible to go to the Ball," Mary said. "All St. Petersburg will be going!"

"His Highness does not consider it safe," the Major-Domo said firmly.

He bowed politely and left the room.

"This is a deliberate fabrication by the Prince!" Mary said furiously. "He is trying to prevent me from going only because he is jealous of Ivan. I can assure you that I am not listening to his croakings of danger. This Ball is being given for me and I intend to be there!"

"How can you if the Prince has forbidden it?" Alida asked.

Mary looked at the clock.

"Ivan should be here at any moment," she said, "and whatever the Prince may have said, I have every intention of going with him to the Ball."

"But you cannot do that!" Alida cried. "You know as well as I do, Mary, that you cannot ignore the Prince, the man you are to marry! If he says it is dangerous to go to the Benkendorf Palace, then the Grand Duchess will agree with him."

She paused and walked to the window.

"I see," she said, "that it has been snowing since we came back from the Winter Palace. By now the roads outside the City may be impassable."

"That is not the reason the Prince is trying to stop me," Mary replied angrily, "and I am going as soon as Ivan arrives."

As she spoke she pulled the bell.

It was only a moment before a footman who was habitually in attendance upon them appeared.

He understood a little French and Mary spoke to him in that language.

"Let me know as soon as His Excellency Count Ivan arrives. Inform no-one else but me. Do you understand?"

"*Je comprends, Ma'm'selle,*" the footman replied.

"Nobody is going to prevent my going to that Ball," Mary said to Alida, "and you must come with me."

"No, Mary, I cannot do that," Alida demurred. "I think it would be wrong . . . very wrong of you to disobey the Prince, and I personally have no desire to court danger unnecessarily."

She thought of what she had endured that morning at the Chancellory and shivered.

"You may be chicken-hearted!" Mary sneered, "but nevertheless you are coming with me."

"No," Alida replied firmly. "If you insist on doing anything so foolish as going to this Ball despite the clear instructions of your future husband, there is no reason to involve me."

"But there is," Mary said. "It is imperative you should be at the Ball tonight."

"Imperative for . . . me to be there?" Alida asked in an astonished voice.

"I was not going to tell you—it was to be a surprise, Alida—but the General is going to ask for your hand in marriage."

For a moment Alida felt that she could not have heard her cousin correctly. Then she managed to ejaculate incredulously:

"The . . . General? Did you say the . . . General?"

"Yes, Ivan's father," Mary answered impatiently. "Ivan was insistent that I should not tell you, but you must see now why it is essential for you to come with us."

"I cannot believe that what you are . . . saying can be the . . . truth," Alida faltered. "But if it is . . . all I can tell you is that I would not . . . marry the General if he were the last man left in the . . . world."

"You would not marry him?" Mary cried. "I always thought you were a fool, Alida, but not a complete idiot! The General will give you a position such as you have never dreamt of attaining."

She paused and added:

"Can you not understand, you half-wit? This will solve many problems where I am concerned! If you are married to Ivan's father—and he has been wanting to get married again for some time—it will be so easy for Ivan and me to see each other."

"Do you think that is sufficient reason for me to marry a man like the General?" Alida asked.

"What do you mean? What is wrong with the General?" Mary enquired. "You are the luckiest girl in the world to have the opportunity of marrying anyone.

You know as well as I do that Papa said he would not inflict you, with your bad blood, on any man."

"I had not forgotten what Uncle Septumus said," Alida answered in a low voice, "but I assure you, Mary, I would rather die an old maid than marry anyone so cruel, so heartless, so repulsive in every way as the General."

"You dolt! You milk-sop!" Mary stormed. "How can you say that? Just think of the alternative!"

She was silent for a moment, which made her next words more impressive.

"If you refuse General Benkendorf, I shall send you home immediately, and I shall tell Papa that you have behaved in such a disgraceful manner that I am ashamed of you."

Mary paused as if to let her words sink in, and then she said:

"You know what sort of punishment you can expect when I tell Papa that."

"Yes ... I know," Alida replied, "but even so, I will not marry the General. I hate him! I hate everything he stands for! I hate Count Ivan too for the way he has behaved with you. It is wrong, Mary, wrong! I will have nothing to do with either of them!"

She saw an expression of rage contort her cousin's features and then Mary reached out to hit Alida hard across the face.

"How dare you speak to me like that!" she raged. "How dare you—a pauper, a gutter-snipe with a mother who was nothing less than a prostitute—refuse the hand of a man who is infinitely too good for you? You will marry him, do you hear? You will marry him whether you like it or not!"

Alida put her hand up to her burning cheek and she was trembling, but her voice was quite steady as she said:

"I am sorry, Mary, but I cannot marry ... the General, whatever you may say, whatever ... arguments you use."

Mary's eyes narrowed. She looked suddenly very like her father as she said slowly:

"Papa was right. There is only one way to treat

anyone like you. There is only one way to get obedience from those who are rebellious."

As she spoke she moved across the room, and as Alida watched her nervously Mary picked up the white
stick which she had brought back that morning from
the Military College.

She had left it lying on a chair by the book-case,
and now, holding it tightly in her hand, she advanced
towards Alida.

"No, Mary! No!" Alida cried. "You cannot ... behave like this to ... me!"

"Will you marry the General?" Mary asked harshly.
"This is your last chance to do so willingly, for I
swear I will make you accept him."

"I cannot ... believe that you are threatening me ...
physically," Alida said with a bravery she was far from
feeling. "But whatever you do, my answer will be the
same! I will not marry such a man! Never! Never!"

She had turned away from her cousin as she spoke
to go towards her bed-room before she felt the full
force of the stick strike her across the shoulders.

She gave a little cry of pain and then, as Mary
struck her again and again, she tried to stagger away.

But the force of the blows brought her first to her
knees and finally, as she heard herself scream and
scream again with the pain of it, she fell forward onto
the carpet ...

"His Excellency is here, M'Lady," the footman's
voice said impressively from the doorway.

Mary threw the stick down beside Alida's prostrate
body.

"I will make your excuses tonight," she said, "and
tomorrow you will accept the General, or I will beat
you until you do!"

She gave a little laugh as she added:

"It will be no hardship as far as I am concerned,
for I find it most enjoyable!"

Alida did not answer.

She heard the door of the Sitting-Room close behind Mary but she lay where she had fallen, feeling
as she had felt after one of her Uncle's whippings—
humiliated and degraded.

She thought of the General, of his hard, cruel face.

"I will die rather than let him touch me," she told herself.

At the same time, she knew how afraid she was of being whipped!

Every nerve in her body shook from the physical agony of the blows, whilst mentally she despised herself for not showing more fortitude, for screaming when a braver person could have controlled herself in shame.

"Oh, Mama! Mama!" she sobbed. "If only I could have died with you! How can I stand up to Mary? How can I endure the pain she will make me suffer if I do not do what she wants?"

She cried despairingly and she was in fact only half-conscious when suddenly she heard a voice exclaim:

"My God! What has happened?"

It seemed to Alida as if she had drifted away into such a darkness of despair that she was hardly breathing. But the Prince's voice brought her back to life.

There were strong hands lifting her to her feet, then as she swayed limply against him, the Prince carried her across the room and set her down gently on the sofa.

"How could this be done to you?" he asked angrily.

Alida knew that he must have seen the stick and the weals on her back! She closed her eyes because she was ashamed.

There were tears on her cheeks and on her long lashes, and he went down on one knee beside the sofa and wiped them away with a soft, white linen handkerchief which he took from his pocket.

He looked at her for a long moment, then, rising to his feet, he walked to the door.

She heard him give an order to the servants outside and then he crossed the room again to stand looking down at her.

"Will you tell me what this is all about?" he asked quietly.

Alida shook her head and he said with a note of command in his voice:

"I need not ask you to tell me who has dared to strike you. The answer is obvious. But why? That is what I must know. Why?"

Again Alida shook her head.

She felt somehow that it would be even more humiliating to tell him that a man as bestial as General Benkendorf wished to marry her.

Even to think of the General made her feel as if she were dragged down into some cess-pool of slime, befouled because he had desired her as his wife.

For a moment she could recall only the look in his eyes and the tone of his voice when he had spoken of the branding, flogging, and *spitzruthen* which he considered an important part of the Army discipline.

Then she forgot about herself in remembering that Count Ivan was attempting to damage the Prince.

She raised her face towards his, but as she parted her lips to speak the door opened and a footman came in with the wine that the Prince obviously had ordered.

The Prince took it from the man and dismissed him, then pouring out a glass of golden liquid he brought it across the room and knelt down once again by Alida to hold it to her lips.

She took a few sips and felt less weak from her suffering at Mary's hand.

At the same time, she now felt a different kind of weakness because the Prince was so near and his arm lay behind her head.

She wanted as she had never wanted anything in her whole life to hide her face against his shoulder and tell him the horror that menaced her.

Then she knew that nothing she suffered was of any importance beside the fact that he might be in danger.

She sipped the wine again and said in a low voice:

"There is . . . something I want to tell . . . you."

"What is it, *Douchka*?" the Prince asked.

She looked at him in surprise because she knew that the Russian word he had used meant "darling," and she felt the colour creep up her cheeks.

"Tell me," he said gently.

"Count Ivan is trying to . . . hurt you," she said hesitatingly. "He has told . . . General Dubbett that you are . . . assisting Mr. Tatkenski to find his . . . mother."

The Prince was suddenly still.

"I think we must speak of this another time," he said very quietly.

Alida knew that he was warning her that it was not safe to talk of Mr. Tatkenski in the Sitting-Room.

"I am . . . sorry," she murmured.

"There is nothing for you to be sorry about," he replied gently. He glanced at the clock on the mantelpiece.

"Dinner will be ready in a few minutes," he said in a different tone. "I am here to escort you and Mary to the Dining-Room, and afterwards I have arranged an entertainment which I think will please you as a small compensation for missing the Ball."

Alida looked up at him with troubled eyes.

"Mary has . . . g-gone," she stammered.

"Where to?" the Prince demanded.

"To the Ball," Alida answered.

"Did you not get my message saying that it was dangerous for you to go there tonight?" he enquired.

"Yes, we received the . . . message," Alida replied, "but Count Ivan called for Mary and she was so . . . anxious to go."

She saw the sudden anger on the Prince's face.

"Are you telling me," he asked, "that despite the message Mary received from me she has set out with the Count for the Benkendorf Palace?"

"You must try and . . . forgive her," Alida pleaded, "but she had been so much looking forward to the Ball. It meant a great . . . deal to her."

"And they are travelling alone—just the Count and Mary, with no escort?" the Prince asked.

"As far as I . . . know," Alida answered. "Why, what is wrong? Is the road . . . impassable?"

"There is nothing wrong with the road as far as I know," the Prince answered sharply, "but I received information that there is a large pack of wolves in the vicinity of the City. To encounter them in a single sleigh could prove disastrous."

Alida sat up on the sofa.

"They must have been gone . . . some time. I do not know . . . exactly how long it has been."

"I must try to overtake them," the Prince said resolutely.

He turned towards the door, but Alida rose from the sofa and ran after him.

"Please!" she cried. "Please take . . . me with . . . you!"

He looked down at her face.

She was very pale from the pain she had suffered and there was a scarlet mark on her right cheek where Mary had struck her. But for a moment she had forgotten everything except her anxiety for her cousin.

She knew that the Prince was resolute and she said pleadingly:

"I cannot stay . . . here alone . . . wondering what has . . . happened."

"Very well," the Prince agreed. "Come with me."

As he spoke he took her hand as if she were a child, and pulling open the door they hurried down the long corridor until they reached the top of the Grand Staircase.

In the Hall the Prince gave a dozen commands in quick succession and the servants ran in every direction to obey him.

Furs were brought by other flunkeys and they wrapped Alida in a sable coat and pulled over her hair the same fur hood trimmed with white sable which she had worn that morning.

There were gloves for her hands and a large muff, whilst her feet were encased in thick boots lined with fur.

The servants opened the front door and she saw that a sleigh was awaiting them outside, with two men on the box.

Even as she went down the steps she perceived coming to join them half a dozen other sleighs, each drawn by four horses.

The Prince assisted Alida into the sleigh. As she leant back against the cushions, the weals on her back were so painful that she gave an involuntary exclamation.

"Are you sure you are wise to come?" the Prince asked.

"Yes! Please . . . take me."

He looked into her face raised anxiously to his, and then without another word he stepped into the sleigh beside her and the servants covered them both with thick rugs.

The Coachman whipped up the horses and they set off at a tremendous pace, and once they were away from the Palace, Alida, moving instinctively nearer to the Prince, whispered:

"Can I tell you . . . now what I have been wanting to tell you . . . all day?"

"Yes, it is quite safe," the Prince answered. "The Coachman and the man beside him are my own servants. They have been with me all my life and are completely trustworthy."

"It was foolish of me to speak in the . . . Palace," Alida said. "I . . . forgot."

"Tell me what is worrying you," the Prince asked gently.

For a second, because he spoke so kindly and the look in his eyes was so disturbing, Alida felt herself thrill with the rapture she had known the night before.

Then resolutely she told herself—she must think of him and not of herself.

"This morning," she forced herself to say, "I was taken to the . . . Chancellory to be . . . questioned by General Dubbett."

The Prince stared at her in astonishment and then he said harshly:

"I cannot believe it! Who took you there?"

"Count Ivan. He called at the Palace very early. I was up and dressed because . . . I could not . . . sleep."

Alida's eyes fluttered as she spoke and she looked away from him.

'He will know,' she thought, 'the reason why I stayed awake.'

"Tell me exactly what happened," the Prince said.

His voice was quiet but the expression on his face told Alida how angry he was.

Slowly she related to him almost word for word the questions that General Dubbett had asked her, and her replies.

"It was Count Ivan who had insisted on my seeing him," she said. "He was trying to . . . implicate you."

"I have news which will please you," the Prince replied. "Mr. Tatkenski and his mother left very early this morning for the Polish frontier!"

Alida gave a little cry of joy.

"They will cross it safely?"

"I am sure of it."

"Oh, I am glad . . . so very . . . very glad! How wonderful of you to save them!"

"They are the fortunate ones," the Prince said soberly. "There are so many others who will never escape."

"They have you to help them," Alida said, "but you must be careful . . . very careful! Count Ivan hates you! Mary has told me so."

"I have known that for a long time," the Prince answered, "and it does not perturb me in the slightest. The Count is determined to retain his Serfs as a boost for his own importance. He has no thought for anyone except himself!"

"That is what I have always felt about him," Alida said, "and he is also cruel and vengeful, like . . . his f-father."

Her voice quivered on the last word and the Prince said:

"Why should the thought of his father trouble you?"

Alida did not answer and the Prince said insistently:

"Tell me, Alida. I have to know!"

"Mary wants me . . . to marry . . . the General," Alida said hesitatingly. "He was to have . . . proposed to me tonight . . . at the Ball."

"My God!"

The exclamation seemed to be jerked from the Prince's lips.

"I imagined many things, but not that!" he said. "Is that why she struck you?"

"She is . . . determined that I shall agree to . . . marry him," Alida faltered.

"Because it suits her!" the Prince said as if to himself. "But I promise you that it will not happen."

Alida's eyes were suddenly full of tears as she looked up at him.

"If I will not . . . marry him," she said, "Mary has threatened to send me home . . . tomorrow, with such a bad report about my behaviour that my . . . Uncle will be . . . angry with me. But even that would be better . . . much better . . . than having to marry that . . . cruel old man."

"Trust me—only trust me," the Prince said urgently.

Alida looked at him in surprise, then she murmured forlornly:

"There is . . . nothing you can do."

"Just trust me," he repeated.

There was something in his deep voice and the expression in his eyes which made her feel as if his arms were round her and he was holding her safe and secure against all the world.

Her face was upturned to his and her mouth was very near to his. She longed as she had never longed for anything before in her life for him to kiss her again.

He drew in his breath. Then as if he deliberately broke the spell which made them both vibrantly conscious of each other he said:

"At the moment we have other things to concern us."

Whilst they had been talking, Alida realised that having crossed the Neva they had passed the few buildings there were on the other side of the river and were now clear of the City and in an empty, desolate part of the country.

There seemed to be only a great expanse of snow, white and gleaming under the moon, which was creeping slowly up a clear sky.

Surprisingly, it was quite easy to see the road

ahead, and the horses had not slackened their pace
since they left the Palace.

"Are the other sleighs just behind?" Alida asked.

She thought that perhaps, if they were alone, they
too would be in danger from the wolves.

"The drivers will try and keep up with us," the
Prince answered with a smile, "but these four horses
are very celebrated for their speed."

Alida looked apprehensively at the white snow all
round them.

"It looks peaceful enough," she said uncertainly.

"Perhaps I was being unduly anxious," the Prince
answered, "but it is always wise to be prepared."

As he spoke he took from beneath the folds of the
fur rug a small pistol which he handed to Alida.

"It is unlikely you will need this," he said, "but I
feel it will give you confidence."

"I was telling the Empress only this afternoon," Alida recalled, "that Papa taught me how to shoot when
we lived in Paris."

"There is only one bullet in it," the Prince replied,
"so keep it for an emergency."

He picked up another weapon and Alida saw that
it was a pepper-box pistol, muzzle-loading, with six
barrels.

The Prince saw her glance at it and said:

"This is one of the fastest-firing guns in existence,
and all my drivers carry one. If we do encounter the
wolves, we will soon dispose of them."

"That is a relief," Alida murmured.

"Did you not know that I would look after you and
keep you safe?" the Prince asked, and there was a
caressing note in his voice that made her feel
strangely breathless.

The weals on her back were beginning to stiffen
and they throbbed and smarted. But at the same time
it was such an ecstasy to be close to the Prince that
nothing else was of consequence.

Any physical pain, she thought, was better than
being parted from him and thinking that he might
have gone into danger without her.

The servant on the box turned and said something

quickly to the Prince. He stood up in the sleigh and
Alida saw ahead of them a forest, the branches of the
fir-trees heavy with snow.

Then as they approached it the sound of pistol-
shots rang out sharply in the silence.

It seemed to Alida that only a few seconds passed
whilst the horses, moving at tremendous speed, entered the wood. Again they heard shots, but now they
were louder.

The moonlight beaming in silver rays through the
branches of the trees made everything seem strange
and ethereal.

In a clearing where the wood-cutters had been a
sleigh stood stationary.

At first it was possible to see only its curved and
decorated back and two people standing up in it
whilst the drivers were firing wildly to the front of
them.

Then as the Prince's Coachman drew his horses
sideways across the path, the moonlight revealed a
great pack of snarling grey wolves devouring the
horses they had pulled to the ground.

There were so many of them that it was impossible
to see anything but the heaving mass of dark fur.
Then Alida saw that Count Ivan was firing a pepper-
box pistol at the beasts while his left arm encircled
Mary.

He shot one wolf after another as they jumped up
at the sides of the sleigh, whilst the rest of the pack
devoured the horses and the carcasses of their com-
rades which had already been killed by the Coachman.

The Prince's man on the box started to fire immediately at the wolves nearest to the Count and Mary,
but even as they were killed their places were taken
by others.

It was obvious to Alida that whilst the hunger of
some of the animals had been assuaged by the meal
they were making, others were still seeking meat.

She rose to her feet to look back through the forest
to see if the sleighs which had been following them
were yet in sight.

At the moment there was no sign of them and anxiously she turned again to see the Prince bringing down wolf after wolf as they leapt, their teeth bared, towards Count Ivan.

As she watched, her heart in her mouth, she saw the Count look at the Prince across the space between them.

His expression was quite clear in the moonlight and Alida could see the glitter of hatred in his eyes, and the sneer on his lips, as if he resented the fact that it was the Prince who had come to rescue him.

Then she held her breath as she saw Count Ivan deliberately lift his pistol in the manner of a duellist, and bring it down aiming at the Prince's heart.

It all happened so quickly that Alida had no time to think.

With a movement of her shoulder she pushed against the Prince so that he took a step backwards to keep his balance, and at the same time she pulled the trigger of the pistol, which she held in her right hand.

She felt the kick as the bullet left it and, almost as if she were watching something happening in a dream, she saw Count Ivan stagger and then slowly fall sideways towards the side of the sleigh.

As he did so, he must have pulled the trigger of his own pistol; for Alida saw the flash and felt something hit her with a force that almost swept her from her feet.

Yet even as she felt the blast she saw one wolf leap higher than the others and drag the Count from the sleigh down amongst them.

As he fell he took Mary with him. There was a flutter of the blue gown and then there was nothing but a great, heaving mass of snarling, hungry, grey animals.

Alida heard a shrill cry of horror and did not realise that it was her own voice.

She knew that she too was falling ... falling into a darkness that seemed impenetrable ... a darkness which swept over her head so that she felt despairingly that it was ... death....

Chapter Nine

There was a sound like the waves of the sea pounding unceasingly, relentlessly, against her consciousness. . . .

Out of the darkness, like coming back through a long tunnel, Alida found herself listening . . . then suddenly, as if a knife had been thrust through her heart, she thought she must be at sea!

She was being taken back to England! She was leaving Russia!

With a little murmur she tried to move, and found that it was impossible; feebly her eye-lids fluttered.

Someone put a hand under her head and she felt something cool against her lips.

Automatically she sipped. Then a gentle voice speaking in French said softly:

"You are safe. *Dormez bien, ma petite.*"

Alida wanted to ask questions, but it was too much of an effort. Darkness was encompassing her once more . . . she drifted away. . . .

Later—was it hours or days later?—she was aware that the gentle voice was still there.

She opened her eyes and saw bending over her a kind face. It belonged to a middle-aged woman wearing a white wimple and a Nun's veil over her head.

Again there was something to drink, and now with an almost super-human effort Alida managed to ask:

"Where . . . am . . . I?"

"You are in a train," the Nun answered. "You are quite safe and we are looking after you. You will soon be well again."

There were a thousand questions that Alida wanted to ask but she could not summon up enough strength.

She felt the softness of the pillow beneath her head, and now the rhythmic sound of the wheels, which she had thought was the pounding of sea-waves, was strange music repeating the same motif over and over again.

'If I am ... in a train ... I cannot be going back to England,' she thought. 'Where ... are they ... taking me?'

Slowly and disjointedly ... she remembered.

Count Ivan's face as he stared at the Prince with hatred ... the movement of his hand ... the pistol which she had known was aimed at the Prince's heart ... her finger on the trigger ... and she could see the Count falling ... falling amongst the wolves ...

"I ... killed him!" she whispered.

Startled at the thought, she tried to sit up. But an agony of pain made her cry aloud.

Voices and soothing hands attended to her ... once again she slipped away into the darkness.

Afterwards, Alida could never remember the sequence of events as she came back to consciousness, only to drift away again.

She was tired, too tired to ask questions! Too tired even to worry as to where they were taking her. She was aware only that the train journey seemed to go on for a long time and then she was moved into a sleigh.

The sleigh travelled slowly ... perhaps so that she should not be bumped about....

There was a ship ... and this time she really did hear waves and the ship's bells ... the sound of feet running about the deck over her head....

Once again she was in a sleigh ... until finally, when she fully awoke to consciousness, it was to find herself in a large room with the sunshine coming through the windows.

There were two Nuns beside her, and by now she knew their voices and the welcome ministrations of their hands.

The elder Nun, who had soothed, comforted, sent her to sleep, and called her *"ma petite"* as if she were a child, was Sister Marie-Claire. Alida felt that she must cling to her for reassurance and a sense of security.

It was Sister Marie-Claire's face which she saw now as she stared at the golden sunshine, and then looked enquiringly round the room.

It was large, light, and exquisitely furnished. Her bed was draped in pale blue, the colour of a Summer sky, and everywhere there were flowers, which scented the air with a fragrance which somehow was a part of her dreams.

"Where . . . am I?"

She was surprised that her voice seemed quite steady. She could recall times when it had been broken and hoarse, days when it had been impossible to articulate a word, let alone a sentence.

"You are in Georgia," Sister Marie-Claire answered. "And this is the Palace of His Highness Prince Vorontski."

At the Prince's name Alida's heart gave a little jump.

"His home?"

"His Highness sent you here to get well."

"I have . . . been . . . ill?" Alida questioned.

She remembered Count Ivan firing his pistol as he fell from the impact of her bullet!

She tried to turn over onto her side, and saw that her shoulder was bandaged.

"You were injured during the fight to save you from the wolves," Sister Marie-Claire said quietly.

Alida was suddenly very still.

"The . . . Prince?" she managed to articulate.

The words seemed almost to stick in her throat.

"His Highness is quite safe," the Nun answered. "He was not hurt in any way."

"And . . . Mary?"

Again it was difficult to ask the question.

"Your cousin is dead," Sister Marie-Claire said very quietly. "May God rest her soul!"

She crossed herself. Then she said firmly:

"Now you must go back to sleep. When you are well enough you will want to hear more about this beautiful Palace, but now—*dormez bien, ma petite*."

It was too much effort to argue, so Alida obeyed. But it seemed, even as she slept, that her dreams were full of sunshine.

She was in the Prince's Palace. He had not sent her back to England, but to his home in Georgia!

Later, when she was well enough to be taken to the window to look out at the incredibly beautiful view, she saw a range of lofty mountains, great lakes lying below them, and a countryside with woods and forests, rivers and streams.

She had known that Georgia, situated in the extreme South of Russia, between the Black Sea and the Caspian and bordering upon Armenia and Turkey, was very different from the rest of the country.

She had not realised until now that the climate was more like that of the Mediterranean countries, nor that the Georgians had joined the might of Russia merely to protect themselves against the onslaught of their jealous, covetous neighbours.

The Nuns in their soft voices told Alida what a long journey it had been from St. Petersburg to the Black Sea, where the Prince's Yacht had met them, and then there had been a short sea-voyage before once again they had to travel by sleigh.

"It is a difficult journey in the Winter," Sister Marie-Claire said, "but *Le Bon Dieu* looked after us and we arrived safely."

Georgia was also under a white blanket of snow, but broken by the forest and lakes and streams, the snow did not seem so overpowering, nor indeed so awe-inspiring, as it had been under the grey skies of St. Petersburg.

"It is very beautiful!" Alida said aloud.

"So is the Palace," the younger Nun, who was called Sister Catherine, cried eagerly. "I did not know so many beautiful things could be collected all in one place."

"It is time Sister Catherine went back to the Hospital," Sister Marie-Claire said with a smile. "She will find it very bare and uninspiring after living in such luxury."

It was some days before Alida could bring herself to ask the questions that was hammering in her brain day and night: "Where is the ... Prince?"

She felt the colour come into her pale cheeks as she spoke because the answer meant so much to her.

"His Highness could not leave St. Petersburg," Sister Marie-Claire explained. "As I expect you know, *Ma'm'selle*, he is fighting as only a great Christian could do, to free the Serfs from the cruelty to which they have been subjected for so many centuries."

"Yes, I know!" Alida said. "But did ... the Prince make all the ... arrangements for my ... journey?"

"His Highness brought you from the forest to our Hospital," Sister Marie-Claire answered. "There was a bullet in your shoulder, which had to be extracted, and he explained that when the wolves dragged Count Ivan from his sleigh, the pistol he carried in his hand went off by mistake."

"Yes ... of course ... that is what ... happened," Alida agreed.

"His Highness was deeply distressed that he and his men could not save the life of your cousin," Sister Marie-Claire went on, "but the two Coachmen were unharmed."

Alida said nothing, and the Nun put her hand over hers.

"Try not to think about it, my child," she said. "It was God's will that you should be safe and that His Highness should bring you to us so that we could nurse you back to health and strength."

"Will ... I be ... disabled?" Alida whispered.

The Nun smiled.

"I wondered when you would ask that question," she answered. "I can tell you in all truth that there is no reason why you should not recover completely from the damage the bullet did to your shoulder. You will always have a scar, but that too will gradually fade."

Alida tried to see the scar the next time it was dressed, but Sister Marie-Claire told her not to look.

"It might distress you, *ma petite*," she said. "A wound is always ugly at first, but Nature is a great healer. You must thank *le Bon Dieu* that you are alive. Nevertheless you must be patient; for you cannot recover quickly from the high fever which accompanied it."

"I am ... grateful," Alida said.

"When you are well again," Sister Catherine interposed, "it will be Spring, and Georgia is very beautiful in the Spring. There are flowers everywhere, as lovely outside in the country as those His Highness grows here in the Palace."

"I want to see the Palace," Alida cried.

"As soon as you are well enough," Sister Marie-Claire told her. "And the prayers we offer for you are more effective than any medicine from a Physician."

Because the Nuns were so kind Alida could feel herself getting better every day.

Besides, secretly in her heart there was an excitement which she could not suppress. She knew that it was anticipation, that she was waiting with every nerve of her body tense for what she dared not express in words even to herself.

She knew only that the Prince had not sent her back to England, that he had found the Nuns to look after her, and that she was in his Palace! In a way, it was almost like being close to him!

Christmas passed, and now the sunshine grew warmer day by day.

"Soon the snow will be melting," Sister Catherine said.

Already there was less ice on the lakes and the rivers were flowing freely.

When at last Alida could leave her room the two maids opened the big wardrobe doors. She expected to see her drab grey dresses hanging there.

Instead there were gowns in all the colours she had longed to possess—blue, yellow, green, pink, and white.

"Are ... they ... mine?" she stammered.

The maids had very little English.

"Come—St. Petersburg—" one explained with an expressive wave of her arm.

Only the French dress-maker, who had Alida's measurements, could have made the gowns, in expensive and beautiful materials, so exquisitely and to fit her so well.

'He was ... thinking of me!' she thought to herself.

Everywhere in the Palace there was something to bring the Prince's presence to her so vividly that he might have been standing beside her.

There was not the overwhelming grandeur of the Michailow Palace. There was not the gigantic impact of size and importance the Winter Palace had upon those who visited it.

But Alida knew that all those who had ever lived in this lovely building had been happy.

There seemed always an echo of laughter in the flower-filled rooms, in the passages which were not so long that one felt they were endless, and in the Salons, which despite being furnished with priceless treasures had a feeling of homely cosiness about them.

Unlike the Palaces and houses in St. Petersburg, there was not one open English fire but many, whilst the great tiled stoves kept the place so warm that Alida needed little more than one blanket to cover her at night.

Finally the day came when she could be taken out for a sleigh-ride.

"We must go slowly," Sister Marie-Claire admonished the Coachman.

He was an oldish man with twinkling eyes and a smiling face which Alida found was characteristic of all Georgians. They were quite different to look at, she noticed as they journeyed along the roads, from the Russian peasants.

The men were slim, dark, and handsome—their features often proclaiming their Greek or Persian ancestry. The women, as beautiful as those in St. Petersburg, appeared here always to be laughing.

When they drove through a little village invariably

there was the sound of laughing and voices singing lustily.

"The Georgians have been Christians since the Fourth Century," Sister Marie-Claire said proudly. "They are tolerant and broad-minded."

"They love sport, music, and the Ballet," Sister Catherine chimed in.

"The Ballet," Alida repeated softly, thinking of her mother.

There was obviously here none of the fear which made every Russian in the North glance over his shoulder to see if he was being spied upon.

The Georgians walked with a confidence which came from knowing that they were a free people.

"Perhaps Russia can be like this when the Serfs have been set free," Alida said aloud.

Some children were waving to them as they passed, and two men hauling a log of wood shouted a cheery greeting to their Coachman.

"One can only pray that might be possible," Sister Marie-Claire replied.

But even as she spoke, Alida knew that she was doubtful whether Russia would ever escape from the domination of its Aristocrats, the power of the Secret Police, and the severity which had become a way of life.

Soon Alida could use her arm and the bandages were at last removed.

There was only a red scar to show where the Count's bullet had struck her, and she found that, whilst Georgia had healed her wound, it had also healed her mind.

She no longer awoke in the night remembering the horror of seeing the Count stagger when she had shot him, or the wolves reaching up to drag him and Mary down into the snarling pack. . . .

At first, although she tried not to think about the scene, it was always there, a picture of horror ingrained upon her mind!

She had thought she could never forget, but Nature is kind and soon the sharpness of the memory began to fade.

Alida found that she could think almost dispassionately of what she had done and face the truth—that if she had not shot the Count, the Prince would have fallen dead beside her.

In throwing herself against him she had saved his life, at the cost of she herself being wounded.

"It would have been better for me to have died than that all his work should have been wasted," Alida told herself.

If the Count had been able to oppose the emancipation of the Serfs without the Prince as his adversary, there was every chance of his being successful.

She knew when she thought of it that in fact she would gladly have given her life for the Prince.

He was of so much importance in the world and his influence was so necessary that no sacrifice mattered beside the fact that he should go on with his self-imposed task.

Then, like the sweet strains of music, the thought came into her mind that now he was free!

"I must not think of it," she told herself. "It is so wrong ... and presumptuous on my part. How can I mean anything to him? How indeed, after the death of Mary in such terrible and tragic circumstances, could he ever publicly turn to me?"

It was then that she felt something like despair.

Perhaps the Prince had sent her to his home in Georgia only because he was sorry for her, because he realised that she had saved him from the bullet which would have killed him, and therefore felt some sort of obligation.

Yet her heart would not believe the logic of her brain.

She could hear his voice as he called her *"Douchka."* She could still feel the wonder and rapture of his lips after they had danced together in the Armoury.

"I love him! I love him!" Alida whispered as she moved round the Palace and touched with gentle fingers the objects she was sure he had touched.

She longed, when no-one was looking, to kiss the pictures of him which hung on the wall, or the miniature which stood on an inlaid *secretaire* which she felt must have been used by his mother.

Then one day, as they were returning from a long drive, they came by a different route.

Suddenly, only a mile away from the great white Palace which seemed to dominate the landscape, there was another building.

It was not very large but exquisite in its architectural proportions.

It stood in the valley, its windows facing out towards Dixlos, the great mountain which was at the end of the long range of high-peaked mountains which sheltered Georgia from the sharp winds of Russia.

The building was so beautiful, with a round silver dome, and two pointed marble towers on either side, that Alida looked at it almost breathlessly.

"What is that place?" she asked the Nuns. "I have never seen it before."

"That is the Palace Angeloychik," the Sister answered. "The name means 'My Angel.'"

She gave a command to the Coachman as she spoke and he drew the horses to a stand-still so that Alida could look at the little Palace.

"Who lives there?" she asked.

"No-one," Sister Marie-Claire answered. "It was built by His Highness in memory of his mother, whom he adored."

"Can we see inside?" Alida asked.

The Nun shook her head.

"No-one is allowed in. His Royal Highness built it after his mother's death and put into it, I understand, everything she treasured most. The old servants who had always served her work there, and the Prince, so they tell me, stays there for a few days every month when he is at home."

Sister Marie-Claire smiled.

"Of course, the stories about it make one curious and they tell me that the flowers in the Palace Angeloychik are more beautiful than those in Paradise!"

"The Prince must have loved his mother very deeply," Alida said.

"From all I have heard," Sister Marie-Claire replied, "she was a very wonderful person. Everyone loved her. The servants in the Palace speak of her with a reverence as if she were a Saint."

It was a week later when Alida rose in the morning to put on one of the beautiful gowns in the colours which she loved.

While the maids were dressing her the two Nuns came into her bed-room, wearing their thick woollen cloaks.

"Are we going driving?" Alida enquired.

"We have come to say good-bye, *Ma'm'selle*," Sister Marie-Claire answered.

"Good-bye?" Alida exclaimed.

"The sleigh is taking us across country to the Black Sea," the Sister explained, "where, we understand, His Highness's Yacht will be waiting for us."

"But why are you leaving?" Alida asked in bewilderment.

"Because now you are well, *Ma'm'selle*, and you no longer have any need of us," Sister Marie-Claire replied.

"But I do not want you to go," Alida cried almost like a child.

"I understand you will not be alone," Sister Marie-Claire said with a smile, "and we have our work to do. The Hospital is short-handed without us, and so, though it is sad for us to say farewell, we must not linger even though we would like to do so."

"But this is so unexpected!" Alida said, looking from one to the other uncertainly.

"It is a surprise for us too, even though we knew it must happen someday," Sister Marie-Claire replied. "But all the arrangements are made, and we are very grateful for such kindness and such condescension.

"It is not usual, as I am sure you know, for us to be treated as we have been here! And I know we will be well looked after on our return journey."

"You said that I would not be alone?" Alida asked in a low voice.

"You can be well assured of that!" Sister Marie-Claire said with a little smile.

She curtseyed and held out her hand, but Alida flung her arms round the Nun's neck and kissed her on both cheeks.

"You have been so very kind, so sweet to me! I can never thank you enough, nor shall I ever forget you."

"And we shall never forget you, *ma petite*," Sister Marie-Claire replied. "We shall pray for you always, and we know, we are quite certain of it, Sister Catherine and I, that you will find happiness."

Alida kissed Sister Catherine also and then the two Nuns left her and she was alone.

She finished dressing and went downstairs.

She had a feeling as she wandered round the warm Palace as if a chapter of her life had closed and a new one was about to begin.

There was a breathless sense of anticipation, of waiting, not with anxiety but with an exquisite certainty that something wonderful was about to happen.

After luncheon, at which she was waited on with every possible attention by the Prince's servants in their green livery, she went upstairs to rest, as she knew Sister Marie-Claire would wish her to do.

She thought she would not sleep, but perhaps because she was so excited she slipped away into a dreamless slumber.

She slept so long that she was still lying on her bed when the maids brought her afternoon tea, English-fashion, on a tray.

"I must get up," Alida remarked.

She had learnt enough Russian by now to be able to talk with the two maids who habitually attended her. What they did not understand, they said with mime.

The older maid, who was called Olga, shook her head.

"No, Your Excellency, there is no hurry. I will bring your bath, and there is a special gown for you to wear tonight."

Alida sat up in bed.

"A special gown? What do you mean? Who brought it?"

Her questions were too quick for the maid to understand.

Instead, she went from the room to return carrying the most lovely gown that Alida had ever seen!

It was white, but very different from the dress which she had worn at the Grand Duchess's Ball. This was of white gauze, embroidered all over with tiny flowers in *diamanté* and pearls.

Alida took one look and knew that they represented the star-shaped orchids which the Prince had told her she resembled.

It was a gown that must have taken weeks and weeks of patient stitching, and it was so lovely that when finally she put it on and looked at herself in the mirror, she felt she should be framed in a picture.

After the maids had arranged her fair hair in ringlets, they brought her not orchids, as Alida had half-expected, but a tiara of diamonds.

For a moment she stared at it speechless, then she realised that it was fashioned in the form of a wreath of blossoms, the flowers moving and glittering in the lights seeming almost real.

The maids set the tiara carefully upon her head, and now Alida was not surprised when they brought her a lace veil as fine as a cobweb.

They did not put it over her face in the English fashion, but let it fall softly on either side of her head.

It covered her glistening gown to the floor and gave her an ethereal look, as if she were a nymph rising from the mists over a lake.

When she was ready and took one final look at herself in the mirror she saw that her eyes were very wide and almost purple in their depths, and yet shining with a strange excitement.

She felt herself tremble.

The maids led her to the top of the staircase and she descended, expecting to find the Prince waiting for her in the Hall. But there was only a servant there holding a sable-fur cloak.

For the moment she was bewildered and then she understood!

The sleigh that was waiting for her was a covered one, almost like a carriage, so that there was no need for her to wear anything over her head or to have fur boots placed on her feet.

There was a foot-warmer on which she could rest her little satin slippers. A sable rug covered her gown.

As soon as Alida entered the sleigh, the horses set off. She knew now where she was going, and she felt an almost indescribable excitement, so that she could only clasp her hands together and pray that she was not dreaming.

The servants were waiting at the door of the Palace Angeloychik to escort her into the Hall.

Still there was no sign of the Prince, but a Major-Domo resplendent in a gold-braided uniform led her down a passage which was bordered with flowers.

Then, before they reached the doors ahead of them, Alida heard the soft music of an organ and knew where she was going.

The Chapel was hung with superb silver lamps that were traditional in a Greek Orthodox Church, but Alida had eyes for only one person—a man who was waiting for her just inside the door.

When she saw the Prince she stood still and it seemed for a moment that neither of them could move. Then her hands were in his and he raised them to his lips.

Singing had begun, the sweet clear voices of young boys, but they could not be seen. Three Priests, in magnificent vestments, were standing in front of the Altar.

Then two acolytes in heavy lace cassocks placed in Alida's and the Prince's hands long lighted candles.

The words of the Wedding-Service were in Latin but a Priest with a long beard and a kind face translated the words for Alida as she repeated her marriage-vows.

She knew as she spoke them that they dedicated her for all time to the man at her side.

Their hands were joined and the Prince put a ring on her finger. Then two jewelled crowns were brought from the Sanctuary.

These, Alida knew, were the Nuptual-crowns, and both she and the Prince kissed them reverently before they were held over their heads whilst prayers were said.

A Priest covered their hands with one of the silver bands of his robes.

When he turned from them to kneel at the Altar, Alida heard the Prince say quietly:

"You are now my wife."

He rose to his feet, helped her to hers, and kissed both her hands one after the other, his lips lingering for a moment against the ring he had just put on her third finger.

And then he led her from the Chapel and back along the passage until a flunkey opened the door of a Salon and they entered it.

The room was filled with white flowers, but Alida had eyes only for the Prince.

She looked up at him, saw the expression on his face, and felt as if her heart stopped beating with the sheer wonder of it.

"You are well again?" he asked in his deep voice which said so much more than mere words.

"I am . . . well," Alida answered. "But why did you not . . . tell me we were to be . . . married?"

He smiled.

"There is an English superstition that the Bride must not see her Bride-groom on their Wedding-Day until she reaches the Altar," he answered. "I only arrived this morning, but I could not wait until tomorrow to make you mine."

She felt herself quiver and he continued:

"Come, our Wedding-Feast is waiting for us, but there are no other guests, no spectators. All this has to be done very quietly and secretly, my darling, because, as I am sure you realise, after what has happened I would not be expected to marry for at least a year."

Alida did not answer. He gave her his arm and

they moved from the Salon into a place which made
her gasp with astonishment.

She had been told of the gardens which existed inside houses in Russia, but she had never seen one.

This was a garden such as she had never dreamt
was possible.

It was a grove of orange trees in full blossom.
White and utterly lovely, they stretched as far as she
could see, and under their feet in the green grass,
which might have been an English lawn, there was a
profusion of white violets.

The Prince, seeing her astonishment, said quietly:

"Their scent has always reminded me of you. They
were also my mother's favourite flower."

It was all too beautiful for expression, and now Alida could see through the orange trees against what
must be the wall of this magical garden that there
were Madonna lilies and white hyacinths.

Also what she had not realised at her first glance
was that, by some strange and ingenious arrangement
of lamps such as the Grand Duchess had told her the
Prince had installed at the Winter Palace, the garden
seemed lit with sunshine.

It was soft and diffused and yet it seemed to Alida
as golden as the happiness within her heart.

Under the orange trees, their blossoms falling on
the white lace cloth, there was a table laid for dinner.

Afterwards Alida could never remember what she
ate or drank. She knew only that the food tasted like
ambrosia and the golden wine with which the servants filled her glass could only have been the nectar
of the Gods.

All she could think was that she was close to the
Prince. His eyes were looking into hers and she could
talk to him as she had longed to do.

"If you are wondering why I have been so long in
coming to you, my sweetheart," he said, sensing her
thoughts, "I cannot tell you what an eternity it has
seemed to me. But I could not leave St. Petersburg
until the Committee had finished their deliberations.

"They have finished?" Alida asked.

He smiled.

"The Delegates have all gone home—we have won!"

"Won!" Alida cried.

"The Delegates voted and the final decision was in favour of the Serfs being given their freedom."

"Oh, I am glad! So very, very glad!" Alida exclaimed.

"The Tsar has now given the Lawyers until October to edit all the findings and prepare a Statute. He will sign it early in 1861."

"You must be so proud . . . so very, very proud!"

"I am proud, and at the same time glad that, now that my duty is done, I can lead my own life amongst my own people," the Prince answered.

His eyes were on hers as he added softly:

"I can also be with my wife."

Alida blushed a little shyly and he went on:

"Now at last I can tell you that I loved you from the first moment that I saw you."

"And . . . yet you would have . . . married Mary," she murmured.

She could not help her reply.

Whilst she loved him overwhelmingly, the hurt was still there that however great their love might be, he would have done the honourable thing and married her cousin, because it was expected of him.

The Prince reached across the table and put his hand on hers.

"I had a feeling you would think that," he said. "Look at me, Alida. There is something I want to tell you."

She looked at him wonderingly and he asked:

"Will you believe me?"

"I will always believe anything you tell me."

"Do you really mean that?"

"I mean it."

"Oh, my *Douchka*, my little flower, you are so utterly perfect in every way!"

She felt herself thrill at the note in his voice and the expression in his eyes. Then he said firmly:

"You have to believe me when I tell you I would not have married Mary. From the first moment I saw you I knew you were the person I had been looking for all my life, who I knew must exist somewhere in the world, if only I could find her.

He paused for a moment and then went on:

"It is not only because you remind me of my mother, whom I adored, but because you are you! Because there is something in me that reached out towards you and which was greater and more powerful than either of us."

"I felt that . . . too," Alida whispered.

"I knew you did, my precious one, and now your heart is my heart, your soul my soul! Whatever difficulties we may encounter, we have each other."

His fingers tightened on hers as he went on:

"You were as aware as I was that because I had been persuaded to agree to marriage with someone who had been described to me as the most beautiful girl in England, I was in honour bound."

"I did . . . realise that," Alida replied, remembering the hopelessness of her despair.

"And so, when I knew I loved you, and that you must be my wife whatever the consequences," the Prince went on, "I spoke to the Tsar."

"You . . . told His Majesty about . . . us!" Alida exclaimed.

"I told him, my love, for you are my whole life," the Prince replied. "The Emperor was very understanding. As I expect you have already been told, His Majesty himself is very much in love."

"But what did he . . . say about . . . us?" Alida enquired.

"He said there must be no scandal and that it would be unthinkable for me to refuse to marry Mary."

The Prince paused.

"I knew that her affections were otherwise engaged, but she could not marry Count Ivan, as he was already married."

"So what could . . . you have done?" Alida asked.

"It was the Tsar who thought of a solution," the Prince answered. "He said that if, despite her obvious affection for the Count, Mary still intended to become my wife, he was prepared to send me into exile."

Alida gave a startled exclamation.

"But that would have meant . . . disgrace!"

"It would certainly have appeared so," the Prince answered. "But I felt quite sure that were I no longer *persona grata* at Court, your cousin would not then wish to become my wife."

Alida knew that that was true. Mary would not have had the slightest interest in the Prince if she had to leave St. Petersburg, if he was no longer spoken of with respect and was socially disgraced.

"But I was quite sure," the Prince continued very softly, "that in those circumstances, if I had asked you to do so you would have come with me."

"You know I . . . would," Alida answered. "I would go anywhere with you . . . anywhere in the world. I thought once that I would be happy living in a garret, if I was with somebody I loved."

"And you would have been happy with me?" the Prince insisted.

"So very . . . very happy," she whispered.

"And now we are together," the Prince said. "I want your help, my darling, in all the many things I shall try to do for my own people. I want your understanding and I want your inspiration."

He hesitated a moment, and then he said:

"It is difficult for me to explain to you what it means to have you with me in this Palace, which I built in memory of my mother. It is, I believe, the only place in the world worthy of you and your flower-like beauty."

"You are . . . frightening me," Alida protested. "I have heard how much everybody adored your mother and what a wonderful person she was. How can I ever try to be like her?"

"She loved me," the Prince said simply, "and all I ask is that you should love me too! I want your love and that you will let me teach you about love. I think in the last few years love is something you have not known."

Alida drew a deep breath.

Just for one moment she remembered the grey

harshness, the misery, and the cruelty she had endured at the Castle!

Then she knew it was all in the past and the future was as golden as the sunshine coming through the orange blossom with the petals falling softly on them both as they talked together.

"I love you!" the Prince said. "God, how I love you!"

The passion in his voice made Alida drop her eyes and the colour rose in her cheeks.

"I have something to show you, my darling," he said, "and as it is outside, I suggest you would be more comfortable without your veil, and perhaps without your crinoline. There are maids waiting for you in the next room."

Obediently, Alida rose to her feet. The Prince escorted her to a door and she found herself in a beautiful little Ante-Room where there were the two maids who looked after her at the Palace.

They knelt down and kissed her hand and she knew that they were pledging her their devotion and service now that she was married.

Then quickly they took off her tiara and long veil and undid her beautifully embroidered gown.

Instead, to her surprise, they dressed her in a Grecian robe of white silk. It was, Alida thought, reminiscent of the Prince's Greek ancestry.

When she realised that its classical lines made it seem rather scanty and it was cut very low in the front, she felt shy.

Then the maids brought an enormous cloak of white foxes, which they set upon her shoulders.

Wondering, but knowing that there was no point in asking questions, Alida went from the room to find that the Prince was waiting for her.

He too had changed, discarding the Military uniform with its many diamond decorations he had worn for his marriage.

He was now wearing just a simple, long, white brocade tunic which had the high collar that so enhanced the appearance of the Russian men.

He looked at Alida for a moment and there was a faint smile on his lips as he said:

"You are my Snow Princess!"

"Where are we going?" she asked.

"You will see in a moment," he answered. "It is a surprise."

The servants brought her a hood of white velvet also trimmed with white fox fur and the Prince himself set it on her head. He tied the ribbons which fastened it beneath her small chin.

"My dream come true!" he said in his deep voice, and she felt herself thrill at the passion in his eyes.

He led her through the orange-blossom trees until surprisingly they came upon an enormous sleigh.

It was quite the strangest sleigh Alida had ever seen: carved, gilded, and decorated with strange devices, it might have been part of a fairy-tale.

The normal, high-curved back was there, but there was no box for the Coachman or shafts for the horses, only more carving and gilding.

The sleigh was lined with white satin and filled with soft white cushions.

When the Prince had helped Alida into it, she realised that her legs could stretch straight out in front of her and the bottom of the sleigh was heated.

'It is almost like a bed,' she thought and blushed.

The servants helped the Prince into a coat of black sable and he set a sable hat on his head which made him look incredibly handsome and attractive, and at the same time gave him a slightly raffish appearance which Alida had never noticed in him before.

Then he sat beside her and the servants covered them first with a white satin rug, then with one of ermine, and a third made entirely of white foxes.

There was a huge muff of the same fur, into which Alida put her hands, and now she saw in front of them, just beyond the last of the orange trees, curtains of white satin embroidered with stars.

These were pulled aside, two great glass windows were opened, and unseen hands pushed them out into the garden.

It was a moonlit night, and although it was cold it

was not the bitter frost-biting cold of St. Petersburg. It was more the cold of an English Winter with a touch of frost.

Alida heard the windows close behind them and they were alone under a starlit sky in which the moon was not yet full, but a crescent that glowed against the sable Heavens.

The Prince turned towards her and put his arm round her. He drew her close to him and she felt his hand covering hers inside the muff.

As he stroked her fingers, pressed his palm against hers, and caressed the softness of her skin, she felt herself thrill and thrill again.

Now Alida was aware of music, there were stringed instruments, not one or two, but a whole Orchestra of them, and they were playing the waltz to which she and the Prince had danced together in the Armoury.

She looked up at him and realised that his face was very close to hers.

"It is very ... beautiful," she stammered, finding it hard to speak because of his nearness and the touch of his hand.

"Look at the mountain, my precious heart," he said.

She obeyed him wonderingly, not quite certain what was happening but utterly and completely content because she was beside him.

Then as she looked towards the great mountain silhouetted against the starlit sky she saw high up on the side of it, almost at the top, the glimmer of a light.

It was very small, faint, and far away, and for a moment she thought she must have been mistaken.

Then there was another light and another coming down the mountain until, as she watched, the lights seemed to widen and move more quickly. Streaks of brillance against the darkness.

Soon it appeared to be moving almost like a river and still it grew brighter and brighter, growing nearer and wider as it came.

Now Alida realised that the music was growing louder and had changed from the soft, dreamy waltz to the music she had always expected to hear in Russia.

A music which seemed to stir the senses and arouse something rapturous and unrestrained in the heart of them. Music which expressed for Alida the wild excitement which was quivering within her.

Nearer and nearer the lights came.

Nearer and nearer, until as Alida watched, just in front of them in the garden a huge fire, brilliant golden, burst into flame.

The flames leapt higher and higher, and as she stared at them the dancers came from every side.

There were men and women in their traditional costumes dancing wildly to the music.

It rose in a crescendo of sound which seemed to draw Alida irresistibly, until she felt as if she too danced round the fire.

Because she was so excited at what she saw she held tightly to the Prince's hand whilst she could not take her eyes from the whirling, twirling figures and the leaping flames.

But she knew that he was looking at her face, watching the reflection of the fire glittering in depths of her eyes. Seeing her lips parted with excitement, her little straight nose silhouetted against the white fur of her hood.

"Fire on the snow! I always meant to show it to you, my beloved," he told her.

"I did not ... understand what you ... meant," she said, "when you said that to me as we looked out from the top of the Palace."

"But now you realise that it is possible?" he asked.

"I think ... perhaps you meant it to be ... symbolic," she whispered.

"It is the fire which I hope I can awaken in you, my *Douchka*," he said. "The fire of our love which will burn away all that is cold, cruel, and ugly from our lives and bring us the ecstasy of belonging to each other."

As he spoke, the flames seemed to rise higher towards the stars, and the dancing grew wilder still.

The figures seemed to be flying through the air as they leapt against the background of the fire.

Sometimes there was the sound of a voice shouting in triumph or with the sheer joy of living.

Then as Alida felt her heart was beating in time to the music, as she throbbed with a strange emotion she had never known before, as the touch of the Prince's hand aroused feelings that she could not describe even to herself, she felt the sleigh in which they lay began to move.

Now they were back inside the Palace, there was the scent of violets, and whilst they could still hear the music outside they could no longer see the fire or the dancers moving round it.

Alida looked up at the Prince and realised the lights behind the orange blossom were no longer golden, but now silver like moonlight.

Yet she still could see—or did she merely feel it?— the expression in his eyes as very gently he undid the ribbons which tied her hood round her head.

Somehow the rugs had disappeared and they were covered only with the white coverlet. His coat and fur hat had gone too, and he undid her white cloak.

The excitement of the music and the dancers which she felt that she had shared made Alida's breath come quickly, and she knew that her breasts were moving tempestuously beneath the soft silk of her gown.

The Prince looked down at her for a long moment and then he said very gently:

"You are my heart, my soul, my whole life and—my wife!"

As he spoke he drew the gown from her shoulder and kissed the scar which had been left by Count Ivan's bullet.

"No . . . please!" Alida pleaded. "I do not want you to . . . look at it. It is . . . ugly!"

"It is beautiful!" he contradicted. "It is a decoration of love, my darling. It is a mark I shall always revere because it saved my life."

He kissed it again very gently and then his lips moved lower over her white skin and she felt herself quiver with a rapturous joy which she had never known existed.

"Do I excite you?" he asked.

"You know . . . you do. . . ."

He kissed the little valley between her breasts.

"This is mine—all mine."

His hand caressed her breast and his lips sought the round softness of her neck! Alida thought that the thrills which ran through her body were a part of the flames outside.

As if the Prince sensed her thoughts he said:

"I will teach you, my lovely one, to burn with the ecstasy of love so that there is no longer the coldness of the snow which frightens you but only the heat and wonder of the fire."

His lips were evoking within Alida a wild desire which in her innocence she could not quite understand, and yet she knew she wanted him to go on touching her, to hold her closer still, to possess her mouth.

"Teach me!" she whispered. "Teach me . . . to be and . . . do everything you . . . want of me."

"You are all my dreams come true," he said. "I will love you for all eternity, until the stars themselves fall from the sky."

He kissed her eyes, her forehead, and then her cheeks. She felt herself tremble all over and she wanted desperately something that she could not put into words, and yet her whole body ached for it.

He looked down at her parted lips, at her eyes dark with the awakening of desire, and he said:

"Tell me, my *Douchka*, what I want to hear. Say what you have never yet said to me. Words which I crave for, which are all I need, now and forever."

Alida understood what he asked and although it was hard to speak because her body vibrated with the wonder of the music and of him, she managed to whisper in Russian:

"*Ia . . . vas . . . liouble* . . . I love you."

He drew her even closer to him.

"That is what I have been waiting to hear you say,"

he said. "*Ia vas liouble*, my darling, my flower, my whole world and my wife."

Then his lips sought hers, and to Alida, as the music grew louder, the flames of the fire encircled them and made them part of it.

His mouth, passionate, possessive, compelling, took her captive. She was his, and they were no longer two people, but one for all eternity!

ABOUT THE AUTHOR

BARBARA CARTLAND, the celebrated romantic author, historian, playwright, lecturer, political speaker and television personality, has now written over 150 books. Miss Cartland has had a number of historical books published and several biographical ones, including that of her brother, Major Ronald Cartland, who was the first Member of Parliament to be killed in the War. This book had a Foreword by Sir Winston Churchill.

In private life, Barbara Cartland, who is a Dame of the Order of St. John of Jerusalem, has fought for better conditions and salaries for Midwives and nurses. As President of the Royal College of Midwives (Hertfordshire Branch), she has been invested with the first Badge of Office ever given in Great Britain, which was subscribed to by the Midwives themselves. She has also championed the cause for old people and founded the first Romany Gypsy Camp in the world.

Barbara Cartland is deeply interested in Vitamin Therapy and is President of the British National Association for Health.